Washington Irving, Edward E. Hale

Knickerbocker Stories

from the old Dutch days of New York

Washington Irving, Edward E. Hale

Knickerbocker Stories
from the old Dutch days of New York

ISBN/EAN: 9783337302757

Printed in Europe, USA, Canada, Australia, Japan

Cover: Foto ©Andreas Hilbeck / pixelio.de

More available books at **www.hansebooks.com**

PS
2072
K5
1897

STANDARD
LITERATURE SERIES

Number 23   March 1, 1897

KNICKERBOCKER STORIES

FROM THE OLD DUTCH DAYS OF NEW YORK

BY

WASHINGTON IRVING

WITH AN INTRODUCTION AND EXPLANATORY NOTES

UNIVERSITY PUBLISHING COMPANY

NEW YORK: 43-47 E. Tenth Street
BOSTON: 352 Washington Street
NEW ORLEANS: 714 and 716 Canal Street

Single Numbers, 12½c. Double Numbers, 20c. Yearly Subscription, $1.75

Published monthly. Entered as second-class matter at the Post Office at New York, N. Y., Dec. 26, 1895

PREFATORY NOTE.

THE following collection gives several of Washington Irving's sketches of Dutch life in the valley of the Hudson. These stories we associate with Irving just as we associate stories of Californian life with Bret Harte, or stories of Creole life in Louisiana with Mr. Cable. Irving was one of the first to perceive the possibilities offered to the imagination by the varied phases of American life. But his sketches are scattered about in half a dozen volumes. It has seemed worth while to gather a number together and to call attention to some of their chief characteristics.

The Introduction is mainly on literary and historical points. The map on page 10 gives the situation of the places mentioned on the lower Hudson. For some hints on the study of Irving's style, the teacher is referred to the Introduction to "The Sketch Book" in this series.

EDWARD E. HALE, JR.

CONTENTS.

INTRODUCTION.

INTRODUCTION.

I. BIOGRAPHICAL SKETCH.

WASHINGTON IRVING is famous as our first great man of letters. He was bred to the law, and was at one time connected with the business enterprises of his brothers. But neither occupation was congenial to him. He followed his true bent when he gave himself up to literary pursuits. He was early regarded in America as the greatest genius in letters that the country had produced. He was recognized and warmly welcomed in England also. It was in recognition of his literary reputation that he was chosen to represent the United States in Spain, a country which, as we shall see, his work had greatly celebrated.

Irving was born in New York City April 3, 1783. He was not sent to Columbia College with his brothers, but at the age of sixteen entered a law office to read for the bar. He was of delicate health, however, and could not pursue his studies very vigorously. In 1804 he was sent abroad to gain strength, and passed almost two years in travel on the Continent and in England. Shortly after his return he was admitted to the bar, and took a place in the office of his brother John.

He had already become devoted to literature, learning first the pleasures of reading ; but shortly, through the columns of the "Morning Chronicle," edited by his brother Peter, he tasted the pleasures of writing and publishing. It was by his pen that he became known. In 1807 he joined with his brother William and an old friend and associate, James K. Paulding, in the production of a jaunty little sheet called "Salmagundi," a bright periodical comment on the fashions and follies of the town. The paper was naturally somewhat juvenile, as Irving said later, but it caused a stir and some talk, and was a successful introduction to a literary career. Two years later he made his position sure by the "History of New York, by Diedrich Knickerbocker."[1] This book had an immediate success, and gave Irving a position as the first humorous writer in the country.

In spite of such a beginning, in spite also of the fact that he could not make anything of the law, Irving had no desire at this time to embrace literature as a profession. His brothers Peter and Ebenezer were about forming a partnership for business between England and America, and Washington was admitted to one-fifth interest. It was not a part of the plan that he should devote himself to commerce. But some years after the making of the partnership, namely in 1815, he took the opportunity of a journey abroad and, finding his brother Peter out of health, assumed charge of the English side of the business. Affairs were gloomy; the recent war with England had seriously embarrassed the firm, and, although Washington worked earnestly for two years, it was impossible to get free of difficulty. In 1818 the brothers Peter and Washington became bankrupt. His commercial duties having come to an unfortunate end, Irving turned his thoughts seriously to literature.

In 1819 he sent home four essays, to be published under the title of "The Sketch Book." These were followed by others and published, first in seven separate numbers of three or four essays each, and afterwards (1820) in the form which we know. It was also republished in England. "The Sketch Book" was as successful as "Knickerbocker" had been. It further secured Irving's position in America and extended his reputation in England. Irving now saw that he could readily support himself by his pen.[2] Feeling comfortable as to his future, he remained in England and France, publishing in 1822 "Bracebridge Hall," and in 1824 "Tales of a Traveller," works of the same general character as "The Sketch Book." In 1826 he went to Spain, and was at once fascinated by the character and the romantic history of the country. He plunged into studies on the life of Columbus and the conquest

[1] For the details see p. 16.

[2] To anticipate a little, the English copyrights of the works written during the twelve years that he remained abroad brought him almost $50,000, while the royalties on the American editions must have amounted to a very handsome sum.

of Granada. His friends often asked if he were never going to return to America; but much as he loved his country, he felt that there was so much to be done in Spain that he could not return at once. He published his "Life and Voyages of Columbus" in 1828, his "Conquest of Granada" in 1829, his "Voyages of the Companions of Columbus" in 1831, and "The Alhambra" in 1832.

Of these works "The Alhambra" is a collection of pieces inspired by the ancient Moorish palace which gives the book its name; it has been called a "Spanish Sketch Book." The others, however, were more serious works of history. "Knickerbocker" had been merely a jest. Irving turned now to history, or rather to biography, with a view of reviving the past by the power of the imagination. In this he succeeded. He is not regarded as a great historian, but his biographies have to a very high degree the power of giving life and color to what may so easily be a mere collection of dry fact.

In 1832 he returned to America, where his reputation had continually increased. He had been absent seventeen years. The country had changed much, and he looked about him a little before settling down. What seized most strongly upon his imagination was the great Western country now more and more being settled and explored. He made a Tour of the Prairies himself, and gave that title to an account of the journey published in 1835. In 1836 he published "Astoria," an account of the exploits of the fur companies, which, under the direction of John Jacob Astor, had crossed the Rocky Mountains and made settlements on the Pacific slope. In 1837 he wrote an account of "The Adventures of Captain Bonneville," an enterprising explorer of the same wild territory.

In 1836 he built "The Roost," as is told elsewhere (page 17), and by the end of the year he and his brother Peter were comfortably installed. He continued his literary work: he had already published in "Crayon Miscellany" sketches of "Abbotsford and its Master,"[1] and "Newstead Abbey," as well as "Legends of the Conquest of Spain." He looked forward to writing the life of Washington, but in 1842, just as he had brought himself to a beginning, he was named Minister to Spain. The appointment

[1] Sir Walter Scott had been a close friend to Irving.

was an honorable one, and he passed four years in the country to which he was so much attached.

He returned to America again in 1846, and from this time lived pleasantly at Sunnyside until his death, November 28, 1859. He began at once upon his "Life of Washington," but could not confine his attention to it. He busied himself in 1848 with a revised edition of his works; in 1849 he wrote his well-known "Life of Goldsmith"; in 1850, his "Mahomet and his Successors." In 1855 he collected a number of minor essays under the title "Wolfert's Roost." Finally, in 1855, appeared the first volume of the "Life of Washington." The second and third followed at short intervals, and the fourth in 1857. The fifth and last volume was produced with difficulty. Irving was in bad health and in a somewhat depressed state of mind. The last volume was published, and the work finished in May, 1859—only six months before his death.

II. IRVING'S PRESENTATION OF DUTCH CHARACTER.

We are apt to think of Irving as much for his presentation of Dutch life and character in America as for anything else. Diedrich Knickerbocker, Rip Van Winkle, Sleepy Hollow—these are more familiar names to us than Geoffrey Crayon, Captain Bonneville, or even the Alhambra. And yet it cannot be said that Irving has given us a good conception of the Dutch character. Even on the appearance of Knickerbocker's "New York," there were not a few who were vexed at the character of the Dutch that was there presented, although it was all in fun.[1] Irving himself always regarded it as no more than a joke.

The fact is that Irving knew nothing of the true character of the Dutch. When he wrote "Knickerbocker" he had in mind a conventionally humorous conception of the Dutchman as a stout, stolid, slow, stupid creature who smoked a great deal of tobacco and wore several pair of loose trousers, whose wife had a passion for cleanliness and housekeeping and wore a great many petti-

[1] Mr. Gulian Verplanck, a distinguished man of letters of his day, commented severely on Irving's picture in a paper read before the New York Historical Society. It is to this paper that Irving alludes in the remarks at the end of his introduction to "Rip Van Winkle," written soon after (p. 86).

coats. He did not trouble himself to think whether the picture were correct or not; in fact, he had not the means of gaining the true conception. He used the common notion as a means for making good-humored fun. And almost any one would admit that, although the Dutch character is presented to us by Irving as nothing very great or splendid, yet it is surrounded with an atmosphere of joviality and good feeling which brings it very near to us.

Still Irving wholly neglected the fine side of the Dutch character of that day. At the time of the Dutch rule in New York, the United Provinces (the name of Holland at that time) were one of the distinguished nations of Europe. They had just vindicated their right to national existence in a terrible war for independence against Spain, the greatest power in Europe. They were using their newly acquired independence to become themselves the chief naval and commercial power of Europe, as will be seen later (page 12). Nor were they a nation of traders and sailors only. During the seventeenth century they had one of the world's great painters, Rembrandt ; one of the world's great philosophers, Spinoza; one of the greatest jurists of modern times, Hugo Grotius; the greatest scholar of his day, Salmasius ; one of the greatest scientists, Huygens; one of the great kings of history, William of Orange, afterwards William III. of England, besides a perfect host of lesser distinguished men. In patriotism, in statesmanship, in learning, in art, in commerce, in war, and in all these directions at once, the Dutch of the seventeenth century will stand a comparison with any nation of Europe of their time. It is idle to imagine that such men were merely fat, pipe-smoking, schnapps-drinking creatures, more stolid than oxen, and more stupid than asses.[1]

It is true that the Dutch of the New Netherlands were not wholly representative of the mother country. The Dutch did not throw their whole spirit into the colonization of New York. It is

[1] The teacher who desires to know a little more of the Dutch will do well to read Taine : " Art in the Netherlands," chap. iii. Douglas Campbell : "The Puritan in Holland, England, and America " speaks of Irving's characterization, p. xliv. Mr. Campbell draws a brilliant picture of the Dutch, vol. i., pp. 216-228, and elsewhere in his book. But Mr. Campbell is not a very accurate writer. He says that Irving acknowledged Knickerbocker to be a " coarse caricature." I think this is an error : the expression was used by Verplanck in the address mentioned above.

true that New Amsterdam was at first but a trading station, and that it never really presented the full power of Dutch character. Yet we must not imagine that the Dutch element in American life

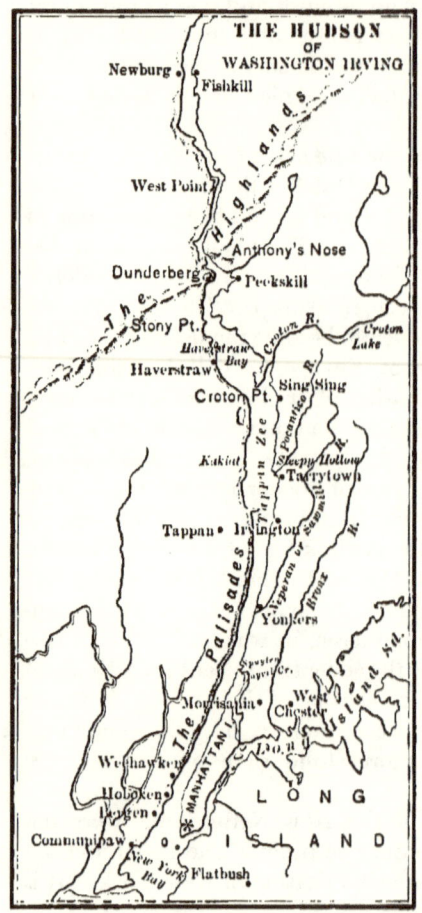

merely sunk below the surface into a torpid, dead-and-alive existence, such as Irving presents to us in his description of Sleepy Hollow. The Dutch in America were cramped by the unwise commercial regulations of the day; they were not allowed self-government; they suffered from incompetent directors sent out from Holland by a company which at first was far too intent on gain. The Dutch in New York had by no means the free development which the New Englanders enjoyed. But in such opportunity as they did have, their national power shows forth to some degree at least, and the great State which they founded has never been wholly forgetful of its founders.

Let us remember, then, that what Irving says of Dutch character is largely made up out of his own head. When he wrote "Knickerbocker" he was a young man writing for his own amusement and that of the public. He had no idea that he was writing anything that would endure and be criticised a hundred years after he had written it.

And, after all, the chief charm of Irving's pictures of the old

Dutch days is not his joke at the expense of the Dutchman. It lies chiefly in the romantic glamour that he has given to the whole Hudson River. He has not only brought out its natural beauty, as you may see in many descriptions which you can realize for yourself whenever you can take a two-days' outing, but he has given it a curiously imaginative, fairy-like character, so that even though now it is so changed, even though we know there is nothing of the old time left, save the great river and the eternal hills, yet as we go up the Hudson to-day, even in the railroad train, there is a certain witchery in the very names of the stations.

This is really the thing we should feel in reading these sketches. It is but a poor thing to do no more than laugh with the clever humorist at his hits on an old popular fancy ; it is something far better to recognize the power and the beauty which the romancer has discovered for us in the great river of eastern New York.

III. The Dutch Period in the History of New York.

It was more than a century after Columbus discovered America before the northern nations of Europe began seriously to colonize the New World. Spain and Portugal at once made settlements in Central and South America, but although some exploration was made of the northern coast, it was not till the seventeenth century that the northern powers began to appreciate the opportunities offered to them.

Spain, the great power of that earlier day, had naturally turned her attention to the milder and warmer regions. The gold mines of Mexico and Peru made her possessions immensely valuable. The northern countries were more severe in climate and had no gold. Yet in time they, too, were settled. When the northern nations began to plant colonies in the new country, France looked farthest north to the regions watered by the St. Lawrence. England came next them on the south, the Dutch were next, then the Swedes, and finally, in Virginia, the English again. We must remember that the Dutch, at first, laid claim to a considerable stretch of country, extending even from the Connecticut to the Delaware.

Holland was at this time (1600–1650) one of the great maritime powers of Europe. By the very nature of their little country a large proportion of the inhabitants lived by some sort of connection with the sea—some by the fisheries, some by foreign trade. The commercial power of the United Provinces was immense. They did business for themselves between the north countries of Europe and the far East, and their ships did a great part of the carrying trade of the other European countries. They were also extending their commercial power by colonization. In 1602 was formed the East India Company, which traded with the countries of the far East from the Cape of Good Hope to Japan, and seized many territories which had belonged to Portugal. The little nation was powerful; its energy, cramped at home in narrow boundaries, flowed abroad on the sea. It was natural that the Dutch should turn their attention to the new world both for trade and commerce. The West India[1] Company, formed in 1621, working for colonial advantage, not only colonized the New Netherlands, but had also settlements and factories in the north coast of South America and in the West India Islands.

It was the voyage of Henry Hudson that started settlement of the country along the great river that bears his name. He was an Englishman in the service of the Dutch Company. In 1609 he sailed up "the Great North River of New Netherland" in search of a passage to Asia, and brought back report of a country rich in furs and fit for settlement. There had been already projects of colonization, and the Dutch soon established themselves in small numbers on the river, but not till 1623 was an important expedition sent out. In that year the West India Company sent expeditions to the South River, now called the Delaware, and the North River, now the Hudson. In 1626 the island of Manhattan was purchased of the Indians for a sum amounting to about twenty-four dollars, and the town of New Amsterdam was settled.

The Dutch power lasted till 1664. At one time or another they held Fort Good Hope and some points on the Connecticut, a good part of western Long Island, the country on the Hudson and a little way west on the Mohawk, some of what is now New Jersey, and several points on the Delaware. But only up and down the Hudson, and in the country adjoining, did they make strong

---

[1] It must be remembered that this name, now confined to a few islands, was in earlier times vaguely given to a great part of the western continent.

settlements, and when we think of the Dutch in America we think chiefly of eastern New York.

At first the Dutch regarded the New Netherlands merely as a means of obtaining a share in the profitable fur trade.   North America existed commercially at this time as a country which produced furs, just as Mexico and Peru had existed as countries which produced gold.   The Dutch at first settled only for purposes of trade.   Here they were at a disadvantage: the English, in New England on one side and in Virginia on the other, had settled in earnest.   But at first the Dutch looked on New Amsterdam and the other towns as mere trading posts.   They did not therefore give the people the independent government which made the strength of New England.   They sent out directors to manage colonial affairs, and the proof of good management lay to their mind in substantial profits.   This was a narrow policy, and hindered the early growth of the colony.

The first director sent out to govern the New Netherlands was Peter Minuit, who came in 1626, and remained six years.   He was followed by Wouter van Twiller, who proved incompetent and untrustworthy.   He was succeeded in 1637 by William Kieft, who was nearly all the time in difficulties with the colonists, the Indians and the English.   He was followed in 1647 by Peter Stuyvesant.

As time went on, the New Netherlands became less and less a collection of trading stations and more and more of a real colony. Settlements extended up the river.   They were made not only under the direction of the West India Company, but in another manner also.   Under the charter of the company several of the directors were allowed to purchase great tracts of land of the Indians, and to settle and govern them independently of the company.   Of these the most noteworthy was Kilian van Rensselaer, whose large territory was in what is now Albany county.   Of this vast estate he was himself the immediate ruler, and received the title of patroon.   Other patroons were also named and, besides the settlements which belonged to the jurisdiction of the company, the country was settled under the authority of these great landed proprietors.

Peter Stuyvesant was the last of the Dutch governors and, on the whole, the best.   He was a man of strong character, upright and just. But he was also imperious and obstinate, and he could never feel that the colonists had any right to self-government or the slightest measure of independence. He was sent to govern them, and he would do it to the best of his ability. The people, however, desired more self-government than the home authorities would allow, and there were frequent misunderstandings.

By Stuyvesant's time the town of New Amsterdam had become a place of some importance. The province had become smaller; that is to say, the Dutch claim to the Connecticut had not been sustained and their settlements on the Delaware had met with a check. The New Englanders had settled permanently on the Connecticut River and all along the Sound toward New Amsterdam. And on the Delaware the Swedes had succeeded in establishing colonies which were continually encroaching on the Dutch. In 1656 the Dutch succeeded in obtaining control of the Swedish settlements, but not soon enough to make themselves strong on the Delaware.

The town of New Amsterdam, however, had flourished. It had attracted not only settlers from Holland more substantial than those who had first come over, but also people from other countries—English, New Englanders, French Huguenots, Germans. The town was no longer a mere trading post, and could not be governed as one. This was recognized by Stuyvesant to some degree: he caused New Amsterdam to be incorporated as a city, with burgomasters and council. Further than this he was unwilling to go, and in his term of office, like Kieft, he had many quarrels with the people. Finally, after constant broils, he gave his consent to a sort of representative government. Had he had time to carry out the experiment, it might have saved the colony to the Dutch for many years.

But the colony was not destined to develop under the protection of the United Provinces. To Holland the New Netherlands were not as valuable as some of her other colonies—Guiana, the Gold Coast, Java. Nor had the Dutch policy built up a strong, independent colony. The English, on the other hand, valued their American possessions, and the colonies of Virginia and New England had by force of events become powerful neighbors. Under these circumstances it was not unnatural that at one time or another the New Netherlands should fall into the hands of England.

There was frequent friction, and in September, 1664, although Holland and England were then at peace, English ships of war appeared before New Amsterdam, and joining the New Englanders who had settled in Long Island, demanded its surrender. Stuyvesant had hardly any soldiers, but he would have defended the town had he been able. As it was, the people, who felt that under English rule they would be granted more independence than the Dutch had given them, insisted on surrender. The English seized the whole province.

The Treaty of Breda in 1667, which ended the war that soon followed, confirmed the English in possession, giving the Dutch the province of Surinam. The name was changed to New York in honor of the Duke of York, except for the territory between the Hudson and the Delaware, which was called New Jersey. New Amsterdam received the name of the province. Fort Orange became Albany, Esopus became Kingston. In 1673 the Dutch seized the province, but were able to retain it less than a year, when it returned permanently to the English, who thereby gained control of the whole coast. The French were to the north, the Spaniards to the south; between Acadia and Florida all was English.

IV. INTRODUCTIONS TO THE STORIES.

Broek.

This is but a slight humorous sketch contributed by Irving to the "Knickerbocker Magazine." It need not be taken as an account of an actual visit; it is really no more than an embodiment of one or two of Irving's fancies as to Dutch character. The calm tranquillity carried to extreme dulness and stupidity, the absurd affectation of shrewdness and wisdom, the cleanliness pushed to an absurd extreme—these elements were the main staple of the Dutch character in Knickerbocker's "History," and these Irving presented in the sketch. It does not appear that Irving ever had any very great interest in the Dutch people. In all the twenty years of his stay abroad he visited Holland but once, so far as I can learn, and then remained but four days. He may of course have visited some village which gave him the main lines of the present sketch, but on the whole we may well regard "Broek" as little more than a fancy.

In "Bracebridge Hall" Irving writes as follows :

"Diedrich Knickerbocker was a native of New-York, a descendant from one of the ancient Dutch families which originally settled that province, and remained there after it was taken possession of by the English in 1664. The descendants of these Dutch families still remain in villages and neighborhoods in various parts of the country, retaining, with singular obstinacy, the dresses, manners, and even language of their ancestors, and forming a very distinct and curious feature in the motley population of the State. In a hamlet whose spire may be seen from New-York, rising from above the brow of a hill on the opposite side of the Hudson, many of the old folks, even at the present day, speak English with an accent, and the Dominie preaches in Dutch; and so completely is the hereditary love of quiet and silence maintained, that in one of these drowsy villages, in the middle of a warm summer's day, the buzzing of a stout blue-bottle fly will resound from one end of the place to the other.

"With the laudable hereditary feeling thus kept up among these worthy people, did Mr. Knickerbocker undertake to write a history of his native city, comprising the reign of its three Dutch governors during the time that it was yet under the domination of the Hogenmogens [1] of Holland. In the execution of this design, the little Dutchman has displayed great historical research, and a wonderful consciousness of the dignity of his subject. His work, however, has been so little understood, as to be pronounced a mere work of humor, satirizing the follies of the times, both in politics and morals, and giving whimsical views of human nature."

Of course this last sentence is the one which gives us the true view of the work. Shortly after "Salmagundi" had come to a close, Irving and his brother Peter conceived a plan for writing a burlesque of a recently published handbook of the city. After they had gathered a considerable material, Peter was called to Europe. Irving thereupon continued the work himself, but quite changed the plan of it: the historical sketch, which was to have been a mere introduction, he elaborated into a complete work. His book he ascribed to a mythical old gentleman named

---

[1] The style of the rulers of Holland was "the High Mightinesses."

Diedrich Knickerbocker, to whom he ever afterward alluded in such terms as are quoted above. "The History of New York by Diedrich Knickerbocker" was published in 1809, and at once became popular in America, and, as time went on, in England as well. In it Irving first developed that half-humorous, half-romantic aspect of the Dutch in America that is so closely associated with his name. The name Knickerbocker became famous, and he himself made use of it afterward. Thus "Rip Van Winkle" and the "Legend of Sleepy Hollow" are both said to have been "found among the papers of the late Diedrich Knickerbocker." In this way did Irving bespeak a welcome for these later works of his, which were similar in vein.

The chapters selected for this book are those describing the city of New Amsterdam in the second book, one from the fourth book, and in the seventh the chapter describing the Hudson. A note on the subject-matter will be found on page 43.

Wolfert's Roost.

These three sketches, pictures of Dutch life on the Hudson in three periods, were published by Irving in the "Knickerbocker Magazine." They have great interest, not only in themselves, but in their connection with the life of the author. Irving always loved the country up and down the Hudson, and often visited his friends who had country seats by the river. When but a boy he had wandered about Sleepy Hollow with his gun. Twenty-five years afterward, on returning from his long stay abroad, he rambled, with one friend or another, among the old scenes about Tarrytown, and explored the old villages among the Catskills. In the summer of 1835, having journeyed here and there about the country, he finally decided to settle down near Tarrytown, where he had already often stayed before. He bought ten acres of land on the river bank. "It is a beautiful spot," he writes, July 8, 1835, "capable of being made a little paradise. There is a small Dutch cottage on it, built about a century since, and inhabited by one of the Van Tassels. I have had an architect up there and shall build upon the old mansion this summer." It was more than a year, however, before the stone cottage was ready, but by Christmas, 1836, he was comfortably settled in "The Roost," as it was called, with his brother Peter. "I am living most cozily and

2

delightfully in this dear, bright, little home which I have fitted up to my own humor. Everything goes on cheerily in my little household, and I would not exchange the cottage for any chateau in Christendom." He subsequently added to the estate, and changed the name from "The Roost" to the better known "Sunnyside." Some time afterward the name of the village near by, "at the request of all the inhabitants except himself," was changed from Dearmain to Irvington.

In "Wolfert's Roost" we have a happy, good-natured wreathing of legend and fancy about the place to which he was so much attached.

The Storm-Ship.

Toward the end of "Bracebridge Hall" Irving introduced a story "from the MSS. of Diedrich Knickerbocker," called "The Haunted House." The tale narrated the adventures of Dolph Heyliger, who lived in New York in the old times. By accident he was carried away up the river in a sloop bound for Albany. They met with a storm, and Dolph was swept into the water by the swinging boom. He succeeded in reaching the shore, however, and in time fell in with one Antony Vander Heyden, a hunter and sportsman from Albany, who took him into his party. As they sat around the camp-fire in the evening, Vander Heyden told the story of the Storm-Ship. The story is not unlike that of the Flying Dutchman, to which, indeed, Irving himself makes allusion. The main lines of the legend will be found on page 71.

Rip Van Winkle.

In the year 1800 Irving made his first journey up the Hudson to Albany. It was "in the good old days before steamboats and railroads had annihilated time and space, and driven all poetry and romance out of travel." He made the voyage in a sloop. The river and the country were a source of immense pleasure to him. Many years afterward he wrote: "But of all the scenery of the Hudson, the Kaatskill Mountains had the most witching effect on my boyish imagination. Never shall I forget the effect upon me of the first view of them predominating over a wide extent of country, part wild, woody, and rugged; part softened away into all the graces of cultivation. As we slowly floated along, I lay on the deck and watched them through a long summer's day, undergoing a thousand mutations under the magical effects of atmosphere; sometimes seeming to approach, at other times to recede; now almost melting into hazy distance, now burnished by the setting sun, until, in the evening, they printed themselves against the sky in the deep purple of an Italian landscape." When in England, sending home the tales and essays which make up the "Sketch Book," recollections of the enchanted mountains came to his mind and he wrote this story. It became an immediate favorite, and has been ever since the best known work of its author. Fifteen years afterward, when Irving returned from Europe, he visited for the first time "the old Dutch villages on the skirts of the Catskill Mountains," looking more closely at the spot he had already made famous.

The story is not entirely the invention of Irving : there are other legends of somewhat similar character. He himself, in the "Sketch Book," spoke of the German legend of Frederick Barbarossa (see p. 60), and there are here and there in the world other stories of those who have been cast into great sleeps, from the fairy-tale of the Sleeping Beauty to the old church legend of the Seven Sleepers of Ephesus. Most nearly like "Rip Van Winkle" is the tale of Peter Klaus, the peasant of the Harz.

But here is proof of the greatness of the writer. It is a story not uncommon ; but Irving tells it in such a way that everybody knows about Rip Van Winkle, though few have heard of Frederick Barbarossa, the Sleepers of Ephesus, or Peter Klaus. It is the genius of the writer which enables him to take stories which might be told by any one, and by his way of telling make them his own. This is what Shakespeare did in so many of his plays (for he rarely invented his plots), and this is what Irving has done in "Rip Van Winkle."

The Legend of Sleepy Hollow.

We have already told how Irving as a boy wandered about Sleepy Hollow. In the story itself he speaks of his "first exploit in squirrel-shooting" (p. 106). We have also seen how, when he returned from Europe, he purchased a place near Tarrytown and enlarged for himself the old Dutch cottage which had belonged to one of the Van Tassels. At a time long before he had any thought of actually settling down, save as a vague wish (p. 6),

while he was living in England, his mind often turning to the
recollection of the scenes of his earlier days, he wrote this "Legend
of Sleepy Hollow," which was published in the sixth number of
"The Sketch Book." "A random thing," he calls it, "suggested by
recollections of scenes and stories about Tarrytown."

At first, the story was based upon "a waggish fiction of one
Brom Bones, a wild blade, who professed to fear nothing and
boasted of his having once met the devil on a return from a nocturnal frolic, and run a race with him for a bowl of milk punch."
But although he first wrote out a sketch of this story, he put it
aside, and merely introduced it shortly (p. 131) in the "Legend"
as afterward written. Later he developed the character of
Ichabod Crane, and Brom Bones became secondary. We can
hardly say that Irving has drawn a very complimentary picture
of the Yankee in the lank Connecticut schoolmaster, and yet,
although we have our laugh over Ichabod, and although there
are certainly some mean points in his character, it would seem
that Irving had a kindness of heart for him. Ichabod Crane
would seem to have been in part drawn from a schoolmaster whom
Irving had known at Kinderhook as early as 1808. Long afterward, Irving wrote to him, recalling the days when they had
been together, and especially mentioning the old schoolhouse, by
that time replaced by a new one. "I am sorry for it," he wrote.
"I should have liked to see the old schoolhouse once more, where,
after my morning's literary task was over, I used to come and
wait for you occasionally until school was dismissed, and you
used to promise to keep back the punishment of some little, tough,
broad-bottomed Dutch boy until I should come, for my amusement—but never kept your promise." It is probable, however,
that his friend Jesse Williams only suggested to Irving some
general outlines, on which he developed the character which we
have in the sketch.

There are other stories of the Dutch life on the Hudson to be
found in Irving's works. We have already mentioned the story
of "Dolph Heyliger" in "Bracebridge Hall." Equally interest-
ing is "Wolfert Webber," one of the stories of the Money Diggers
in "Tales of a Traveller." Also should be mentioned "Guests
from Gibbet Island," to be found in "Wolfert's Roost."

KNICKERBOCKER STORIES.

I.—BROEK: OR THE DUTCH PARADISE.

It has long been a matter of discussion and controversy among the pious and the learned, as to the situation of the terrestrial paradise[1] whence our first parents were exiled. This question has been put to rest by certain of the faithful in Holland, who have decided in favor of the village of BROEK, about six miles from Amsterdam. It may not, they observe, correspond in all respects to the description of the Garden of Eden, handed down from days of yore, but it comes nearer to their ideas of a perfect paradise than any other place on earth.

This eulogium[2] induced me to make some inquiries as to this favored spot in the course of a sojourn at the city of Amsterdam, and the information I procured fully justified the enthusiastic praises I had heard. The village of Broek is situated in Waterland,[3] in the midst of the greenest and richest pastures of Holland, I may say, of Europe. These pastures are the source of its wealth, for it is famous for its

[1] This humorous introduction of the subject is not wholly of Irving's own invention. There was much discussion as to the situation of the Garden of Eden, the earthly paradise, in bygone times. When Irving says, however, that some have thought it might be Broek, he is only in fun.

[2] good report.

[3] Holland used to be a union of seven provinces. None of them, however, was named Waterland. Irving invents the name because the country lies low and is inundated here and there; it also has canals often where other nations have roads.

dairies, and for those oval cheeses which regale and perfume the whole civilized world. The population consists of about six hundred persons, comprising several families which have inhabited the place since time immemorial, and have waxed rich on the products of their meadows. They keep all their wealth among themselves, intermarrying, and keeping all strangers at a wary distance. They are a "hard money" people, and remarkable for turning the penny the right way.[1] It is said to have been an old rule, established by one of the primitive financiers and legislators of Broek, that no one should leave the village with more than six guilders[2] in his pocket, or return with less than ten ; a shrewd regulation, well worthy the attention of modern political economists, who are so anxious to fix the balance of trade.[3]

What, however, renders Broek so perfect an elysium,[4] in the eyes of all true Hollanders, is the matchless height to which the spirit of cleanliness[5] is carried there. It amounts almost to a religion among the inhabitants, who pass the greater part of their time rubbing and scrubbing, and painting and varnishing : each housewife vies with her neighbor in her devotion to the scrubbing-brush, as zealous Catholics do in their devotion to the cross ; and it is said a notable housewife of the place in days of yore is held in pious remembrance, and almost canonized as a saint, for having died of pure exhaus-

[1] The Dutch people are thrifty and economical. Irving constantly makes fun of this trait in very American fashion. Economy, however, is really far more creditable than the wastefulness which is more common in America.

[2] a coin worth about forty cents.

[3] When a country sends forth to other countries more products and manufactures than it buys from them, it is obvious that it will receive in payment more money than it pays out. Then the "balance of trade" is said to be in its favor, for, taking the country all together, there is more due it from abroad than it owes abroad, and money must come to pay the indebtedness. If every one who left Broek came back with more money than he had carried away, it would be as if the balance of trade were always in their favor.

[4] the name given by the Greeks to Heaven. Here used figuratively, like "a perfect paradise" (p. 21).

[5] Notice how often Irving plays upon the idea in the following pages; he speaks of the newly scrubbed pavements, the fresh-painted houses, the "varnished" tree-trunks, and of many other such things. See pp. 23, 24, 25.

tion and chagrin in an ineffectual attempt to scour a black man white.

These particulars awakened my ardent curiosity to see a place which I pictured to myself the very fountain-head of certain hereditary habits and customs prevalent among the descendants of the original Dutch settlers of my native State. I accordingly lost no time in performing a pilgrimage to Broek.

Before I reached the place I beheld symptoms of the tranquil character of its inhabitants. A little clump-built boat was in full sail along the lazy bosom of a canal, but its sail consisted of the blades of two paddles stood on end, while the navigator sat steering with a third paddle in the stern, crouched down like a toad, with a slouched hat drawn over his eyes. I presumed him to be some nautical lover on the way to his mistress. After proceeding a little farther I came in sight of the harbor or port of destination of this drowsy navigator. This was the Broeken-Meer, an artificial basin, or sheet of olive-green water, tranquil as a mill-pond. On this the village of Broek is situated, and the borders are laboriously decorated with flower-beds, box-trees clipped into all kinds of ingenious shapes and fancies, and little " lust " houses [1] or pavilions.

I alighted outside of the village, for no horse nor vehicle is permitted to enter its precincts, lest it should cause defilement of the well-scoured pavements. Shaking the dust off my feet, therefore, I prepared to enter, with due reverence and circumspection, this *sanctum sanctorum* [2] of Dutch cleanliness. I entered by a narrow street, paved with yellow bricks, [3] laid edgewise, so clean that one might eat from them. Indeed, they were actually worn deep, not by the tread of feet, but by the friction of the scrubbing-brush.

The houses were built of wood, and all appeared to have

---

[1] a combination of Dutch and English. *Lust* is Dutch for " pleasure."

[2] holy of holies.

[3] This practice, which seemed humorous to Irving, is not uncommon nowadays. We think it a great advance to change the old cobble pavements of Irving's day for " yellow bricks laid edgewise." The brick pavements of the present are not always so clean as those of Broek.

been freshly painted, of green, yellow, and other bright colors. They were separated from each other by gardens and orchards, and stood at some little distance from the street, with wide areas or courtyards, paved in mosaic, with variegated stones, polished by frequent rubbing. The areas were divided from the street by curiously-wrought railings, or balustrades, of iron, surmounted with brass and copper balls, scoured into dazzling effulgence. The very trunks of the trees in front of the houses were by the same process made to look as if they had been varnished. The porches, doors, and window-frames of the houses were of exotic[1] woods, curiously carved, and polished like costly furniture. The front doors are never opened, excepting on christenings, marriages, or funerals: on all ordinary occasions, visitors enter by the back-door. In former times, persons when admitted had to put on slippers,[2] but this oriental ceremony is no longer insisted upon.

A poor devil Frenchman who attended upon me as cicerone,[3] boasted with some degree of exultation, of a triumph of his countrymen over the stern regulations of the place. During the time that Holland was overrun by the armies of the French Republic,[4] a French general, surrounded by his whole *état major*,[5] who had come from Amsterdam to view the wonders of Brock, applied for admission at one of these taboo'd[6] portals. The reply was, that the owner never received any one who did not come introduced by some friend. "Very well," said the general, "take my compliments to your master, and tell him I will return here to-morrow with a company of soldiers, *pour parler raison avec mon ami Hollandais.*"[7] Terrified at the

---

[1] foreign.

[2] Strangers who enter Eastern mosques are provided with slippers, which they must put on over their shoes. Hence the word "oriental" in the following line.

[3] guide.

[4] In 1795, when, after a short invasion, Holland and Belgium were united to France, which had just become a republic.

[5] a French word meaning "staff."

[6] In the South Sea Islands the *tabu* is a prohibition of intercourse. Any one "taboo'd" is avoided by every one else. The word was new to English in Irving's day, and he used it loosely of this door, meaning that no one was allowed to enter it.

[7] "To talk common sense with my Dutch friend."

idea of having a company of soldiers billeted [1] upon him, the owner threw open his house, entertained the general and his retinue with unwonted hospitality; though it is said it cost the family a month's scrubbing and scouring, to restore all things to exact order, after this military invasion. My vagabond informant seemed to consider this one of the greatest victories of the republic.

I walked about the place in mute wonder and admiration. A dead stillness prevailed around, like that in the deserted streets of Pompeii.[2] No sign of life was to be seen, excepting now and then a hand, and a long pipe, and an occasional puff of smoke, out of the window of some "lust-haus" overhanging a miniature canal; and on approaching a little nearer, the periphery[3] in profile of some robustious burgher.

Among the grand houses pointed out to me were those of Claes Bakker, and Cornelius Bakker, richly carved and gilded, with flower gardens and clipped shrubberies; and that of the Great Ditmus, who, my poor devil cicerone informed me, in a whisper, was worth two millions; all these were mansions shut up from the world, and only kept to be cleaned. After having been conducted from one wonder to another of the village, I was ushered by my guide into the grounds and gardens of Mynheer Broekker, another mighty cheese-manufacturer, worth eighty thousand guilders a year. I had repeatedly been struck with the similarity of all that I had seen in this amphibious[4] little village, to the buildings and land-scapes on Chinese platters and tea-pots; but here I found the similarity complete; for I was told that these gardens were modelled upon Van Braam's description of those of Yuen min Yuen, in China. Here were serpentine walks, with trellised

---

[1] In time of war, soldiers staying in a town or village, are often lodged in the various houses, generally without consent or payment. This is called "billeting."

[2] an old Roman city, destroyed by an eruption of Vesuvius, A.D. 79.

[3] the circumference of a circle: the use of the word here indicates that the old gentleman's outline was almost circular.

[4] living on land and water. Cf. "Water-land."

borders; winding canals, with fanciful Chinese bridges;
flower-beds resembling huge baskets, with the flower of "love
lies bleeding" falling over to the ground.   But mostly had the
fancy of Mynheer Brockker been displayed about a stagnant
little lake, on which a corpulent little pinnace [1] lay at anchor.
On the border was a cottage, within which were a wooden man
and woman seated at table, and a wooden dog beneath, all the
size of life: on pressing a spring, the woman commenced spinning, and the dog barked furiously.   On the lake were wooden
swans, painted to the life; some floating, others on the nest
among the rushes; while a wooden sportsman, crouched
among the bushes, was preparing his gun to take deadly aim.
In another part of the garden was a dominie [2] in his clerical
robes, with wig, pipe, and cocked hat; and mandarins with
nodding heads, amid red lions, green tigers, and blue hares.
Last of all, the heathen deities, in wood and plaster, male and
female, naked and bare-faced as usual, and seeming to stare
with wonder at finding themselves in such strange company.

My shabby French guide, while he pointed out all these
mechanical marvels of the garden, was anxious to let me see
that he had too polite a taste to be pleased with them.   At
every new nick-nack he would screw down his mouth, shrug
up his shoulders, take a pinch of snuff, and exclaim : " *Ma
foi, Monsieur, ces Hollandais sont forts pour ces bêtises là!* " [3]

To attempt to gain admission to any of these stately abodes
was out of the question, having no company of soldiers to
enforce a solicitation. [4]   I was fortunate enough, however,
through the aid of my guide, to make my way into the
kitchen of the illustrious Ditmus, and I question whether the
parlor would have proved more worthy of observation.   The
cook, a little wiry, hook-nosed woman, worn thin by incessant
action and friction, was bustling about among her kettles and

[1] a small sailboat, generally with two masts and schooner-rigged.
[2] the Dutch title for clergyman.
[3] "Truly, sir, the Dutch are great on such foolish things."
[4] as the general on p. 24 had had.

saucepans, with the scullion[1] at her heels, both in clattering wooden shoes, which were as clean and white as the milk-pails ; rows of vessels, of brass and copper, regiments of pewter dishes, and portly porringers,[2] gave resplendent evidence of the intensity of their cleanliness ; the very trammels and hangers[3] in the fireplace were highly scoured, and the burnished face of the good St. Nicholas[4] shone forth from the iron plate of the chimney-back.

Among the decorations of the kitchen was a printed sheet of woodcuts, representing the various holiday customs of Holland, with explanatory rhymes. Here I was delighted to recognize the jollities of New Year's Day ;[5] the festivities of Paas and Pinkster,[6] and all the other merry-makings handed down in my native place from the earliest times of New-Amsterdam,[7] and which had been such bright spots in the year in my childhood. I eagerly made myself master of this precious document, for a trifling consideration, and bore it off as a memento of the place ; though I question if, in so doing, I did not carry off with me the whole current literature of Broek.

I must not omit to mention that this village is the paradise of cows as well as men : indeed you would almost suppose the cow to be as much an object of worship here as the bull[8] was among the ancient Egyptians ; and well does she merit it, for she is in fact the patroness of the place. The same scrupulous cleanliness, however, which pervades everything else, is mani-

[1] a boy who helps in the kitchen.

[2] a vessel like a saucer, but deeper, and having one or two flat ears or handles.

[3] instruments hung in the great fire-places of the old times for suspending pots and kettles.

[4] St. Nicholas is better known by the abbreviation into Santa Claus. St. Nicholas' Day is December 6th, but the sportive ceremonies with which it was celebrated are now transferred to Christmas.

[5] New Year's Day was formerly observed with more ceremonies in New York than elsewhere in the country.

[6] Easter and Whitsunday. Even now one may see " Paas eggs " in the window at Easter, and the " Pinkster-flower " in the woods at Whitsuntide.

[7] the name of New York under Dutch rule.

[8] The Sacred Bull of Memphis was worshipped in ancient Egypt as the image of the soul of Osiris. He was called Apis.

fested in the treatment of this venerated animal. She is not
permitted to perambulate the place, but in winter, when she
forsakes the rich pasture, a well-built house is provided for
her, well painted, and maintained in the most perfect order.
Her stall is of ample dimensions; the floor is scrubbed and
polished; her hide is daily curried and brushed and sponged
to her heart's content, and her tail is daintily tucked up to
the ceiling and decorated with a riband !

On my way back through the village, I passed the house of
the prediger,[1] or preacher; a very comfortable mansion, which
led me to augur well of the state of religion in the village. On
inquiry, I was told that for a long time the inhabitants lived
in a great state of indifference as to religious matters : it was
in vain that their preachers endeavored to arouse their
thoughts as to a future state ; the joys of heaven, as commonly depicted, were but little to their taste. At length a
dominie appeared among them who struck out in a different
vein. He depicted the New Jerusalem as a place all smooth
and level, with beautiful dykes,[2] and ditches and canals ;[3] and
houses all shining with paint and varnish, and glazed tiles ;
and where there should never come horse, or ass, or cat, or
dog, or anything that could make noise or dirt ; but there
should be nothing but rubbing and scrubbing, and washing
and painting, and gilding and varnishing, for ever and ever,
amen ! Since that time, the good housewives of Brook have
all turned their faces Zionward.[4]

---

[1] The word is German. The Dutch
form is *predikar*.

[2] great sea walls, by which the sea is
kept from overflowing the low-lying parts
of Holland.

[3] Holland is covered with canals as
other countries are with roads.

[4] Zion is the hill on which Jerusalem is
built. The name is often used symboli-
cally for Heaven.

II *a*.—NEW AMSTERDAM UNDER VAN TWILLER.

AS DESCRIBED IN KNICKERBOCKER'S HISTORY OF NEW YORK, BOOK III., CHAPTERS II., III., IV.

THE modern spectator, who wanders through the streets of this populous[1] city, can scarcely form an idea of the differ-ent appearance they presented in the primitive days of the Doubter.[2] The busy hum of multitudes, the shouts of revelry, the rumbling equipages of fashion, the rattling of accursed carts, and all the spirit-grieving sounds of brawling commerce, were unknown in the settlement of New-Amsterdam.[3] The grass grew quietly in the highways—the bleating sheep and frolicsome calves sported about the verdant ridge where now the Broadway loungers take their morning stroll—the cunning fox or ravenous wolf skulked in the woods, where now are to be seen the dens of Gomez and his righteous fraternity of money-brokers—and flocks of vociferous geese cackled about the fields, where now the great Tammany[4] wigwam and the patriotic tavern of Martling echo with the wranglings of the mob.

In those good times did a true and enviable equality of rank and property prevail, equally removed from the arrogance of wealth, and the servility and heart-burnings of repining poverty—and what in my mind is still more conducive to tranquillity and harmony among friends, a happy equality of intellect was likewise to be seen. The minds of the good burghers[5] of New-Amsterdam seemed all to have been cast in

---

[1] In 1890 the population was 1,513,301, according to the United States census.

[2] Wouter Van Twiller, the second Director (p. 13), was so called by Irving. See p. 77.

[3] the name of the town until the English, on taking possession, changed it to New York in honor of the Duke of York, the brother of King Charles II.

[4] The Tammany Society had been incorporated in 1805, not long before "Knickerbocker" was published. The first "Tammany Hall" was not built till 1811.

[5] citizens.

one mould, and to be those honest, blunt minds, which, like
certain manufactures, are made by the gross, and considered
as exceedingly good for common use.

Thus it happens that your true dull minds are generally
preferred for public employ, and especially promoted to city
honors ; your keen intellects, like razors, being considered too
sharp for common service.   I know that it is common to rail
at the unequal distribution of riches, as the great source of
jealousies, broils, and heart-breakings ; whereas, for my part,
I verily believe it is the sad inequality of intellect that prevails, that embroils communities more than anything else ;
and I have remarked that your knowing people, who are so
much wiser than anybody else, are eternally keeping society
in a ferment.   Happily for New-Amsterdam, nothing of the
kind was shown within its walls—the very words of learning,
education, taste, and talents were unheard of—a bright genius
was an animal unknown, and a blue-stocking [1] lady would
have been regarded with as much wonder as a horned frog or
a fiery dragon.   No man, in fact, seemed to know more than
his neighbor, nor any man to know more than an honest man
ought to know, who has nobody's business to mind but his
own ; the parson and the council clerk were the only men
that could read in the community, and the sage Van Twiller
always signed his name with a cross.

Thrice happy and ever to be envied little burgh ! existing
in all the security of harmless insignificance—unnoticed and
unenvied by the world, without ambition, without vain-glory,
without riches, without learning, and all their train of carking
cares ;—and as of yore,[2] in the better days of man, the deities
were wont to visit him on earth and bless his rural habitations,
so we are told, in the sylvan [3] days of New-Amsterdam, the
good St. Nicholas [4] would often make his appearance in his

---

beloved city, of a holyday afternoon, riding jollily among the tree-tops, or over the roofs of the houses, now and then drawing forth magnificent presents from his breeches pockets, and dropping them down the chimneys of his favorites. Whereas in these degenerate days of iron and brass,[1] he never shows us the light of his countenance, nor ever visits us, save one night[2] in the year; when he rattles down the chimneys of the descendants of the patriarchs, confining his presents merely to the children, in token of the degeneracy of the parents.

Such are the comfortable and thriving effects of a fat government. The province of the New-Netherlands,[3] destitute of wealth, possessed a sweet tranquillity that wealth could never purchase. There were neither public commotions, nor private quarrels; neither parties, nor sects, nor schisms; neither persecutions, nor trials, nor punishments; nor were there counsellors, attorneys, catch-poles,[4] or hangmen. Every man attended to what little business he was lucky enough to have, or neglected it if he pleased, without asking the opinion of his neighbor. In those days, not dy meddled with concer￢ above his comprehension, nor thrust his nose into other ﹖ ple's affairs; nor neglected to correct his own conduct, and reform his own character, in his zeal to pull to pieces the characters of others—but in a word, every respectable citizen eat when he was not hungry, drank when he was not thirsty, and went regularly to bed when the sun set, and the fowls went to roost, whether he were sleepy or not; all which tended remarkably to the population of the settlement. Every thing went on exactly as it should do; and in the usual words employed by historians to express the welfare of a country, "the profoundest *tranquillity* and *repose* reigned throughout the province."

---

[1] The "good old times" are often called the Golden Age (p. 42); in contrast to it the present is sometimes called the Brazen or the Iron Age by such as like to think that things nowadays are worse than they used to be.

[2] Christmas.

[3] the province, under the Dutch.

[4] sheriff's assistants.

Manifold are the tastes and dispositions of the enlightened literati, who turn over the pages of history. Some there be, whose hearts are brimful of the yeast of courage, and whose bosoms do work, and swell and foam, with untried valor, like a barrel of new cider, or a train-band ' captain, fresh from under the hands of his tailor. This doughty class of readers can be satisfied with nothing but bloody battles and horrible encounters; they must be continually storming forts, sacking cities, springing mines, marching up to the muzzles of cannon, charging bayonets through every page, and revelling in gunpowder and carnage. Others, who are of a less martial, but equally ardent imagination, and who, withal, are a little given to the marvellous, will dwell with wondrous satisfaction on descriptions of prodigies, unheard-of events, hairbreadth escapes, hardy adventures, and all those astonishing narrations just amble along the boundary line of possibility. A ' class, who, not to speak slightly of them, are of a lighter and skim over the records of past times, as they do over difying pages of a novel, merely for relaxation and his cent amusement, do singularly delight in treasons, executions, conflagrations, murders, and all the other catalogue of hideous crimes, that, like cayenne in cookery, do give a pungency and flavor to the dull detail of history—while a fourth class, of more philosophic habits, do diligently pore over the musty chronicles of time, to investigate the operations of the human kind, and watch the gradual changes in men and manners, effected by the progress of knowledge, the vicissitudes of events, or the influence of situation.

If the three first classes find but little wherewithal to solace themselves in the tranquil reign of Wouter Van Twiller, I entreat them to exert their patience for a while, and bear with the tedious picture of happiness, prosperity, and peace, which my duty as a faithful historian obliges me to draw; and I

' The militia of an earlier day were called the "trained bands," or, more shortly, "trainbands."

STANDARD LITERATURE SERIES

KNICKERBOCKER STORIES

FROM THE OLD DUTCH DAYS OF
NEW YORK

BY

WASHINGTON IRVING

EDITED WITH INTRODUCTION AND NOTES

BY

EDWARD EVERETT HALE, Jr., Ph.D.

PROFESSOR OF RHETORIC AND LOGIC IN UNION COLLEGE

UNIVERSITY PUBLISHING COMPANY

NEW YORK, BOSTON AND NEW ORLEANS

Press of J. J. Little & Co.
Astor Place, New York

promise them that as soon as I can possibly light upon any thing horrible, uncommon, or impossible, it shall go hard, but I will make it afford them entertainment. This being promised, I turn with great complacency to the fourth class of my readers, who are men, or, if possible, women, after my own heart ; grave, philosophical, and investigating ; fond of analyzing characters, of taking a start from first causes, and so hunting a nation down, through all the mazes of innovation and improvement. Such will naturally be anxious to witness the first development of the newly-hatched colony, and the primitive manners and customs prevalent among its inhabitants, during the halcyon[1] reign of Van Twiller, or the Doubter.

I will not grieve their patience, however, by describing minutely the increase and improvement of New-Amsterdam. Their own imaginations will doubtless present to them the good burghers, like so many pains-taking and persevering beavers, slowly and surely pursuing their labours—they will behold the prosperous transformation from the rude log-hut to the stately Dutch mansion, with brick front, glazed windows, and tiled roof—from the tangled thicket to the luxuriant cabbage garden ; and from the skulking Indian to the ponderous burgomaster. In a word, they will picture to themselves the steady, silent, and undeviating march to prosperity, incident to a city destitute of pride or ambition, cherished by a fat government, and whose citizens do nothing in a hurry.

The sage council, as has been mentioned in a preceding chapter, not being able to determine upon any plan for the building of their city—the cows, in a laudable fit of patriotism, took it under their peculiar charge, and as they went to and from pasture, established paths through the bushes, on each side of which the good folks built their houses ; which is one cause of the rambling and picturesque turns and labyrinths,

---

[1] a name for the kingfisher. The old legend was that, at a certain time of the year, the halcyon's nest floated on the sea, and that for that time the winds were quiet and the weather mild and delightful. A "halcyon reign" is like a "golden age."

3

which distinguish certain streets of New-York at this very
day.

The houses of the higher class were generally constructed of
wood, excepting the gable end, which was of small black and
yellow Dutch bricks, and always faced on the street, as our
ancestors, like their descendants, were very much given to
outward show, and were noted for putting the best leg foremost. The house was always furnished with abundance of
large doors and small windows on every floor ; the date of its
erection was curiously designated by iron figures on the front ;
and on the top of the roof was perched a fierce little weather-
cock, to let the family into the important secret which way
the wind blew. These, like the weathercocks on the tops of
our steeples, pointed so many different ways, that every man
could have a wind to his mind ;—the most staunch and loyal
citizens, however, always went according to the weathercock
on the top of the governor's house, which was certainly the
most correct, as he had a trusty servant employed every morning to climb up and set it to the right quarter.

In those good days of simplicity and sunshine, a passion for
cleanliness[1] was the leading principle in domestic economy,
and the universal test of an able housewife—a character which
formed the utmost ambition of our unenlightened grandmothers. The front door was never opened except on marriages,
funerals, new-year's days, the festival of St. Nicholas, or some
such great occasion. It was ornamented with a gorgeous
brass knocker, curiously wrought, sometimes in the device of
a dog, and sometimes of a lion's head, and was daily burnished
with such religious zeal, that it was ofttimes worn out by the
very precautions taken for its preservation. The whole house
was constantly in a state of inundation, under the discipline
of mops and brooms and scrubbing-brushes ; and the good
housewives of those days were a kind of amphibious animal,
delighting exceedingly to be dabbling in water—insomuch

[1] See p. 22.

that a historian of the day gravely tells us, that many of his townswomen grew to have webbed fingers like unto a duck ; and some of them, he had little doubt, could the matter be examined into, would be found to have the tails of mermaids —but this I look upon to be a mere sport of fancy, or what is worse, a wilful misrepresentation.

The grand parlor was the *sanctum sanctorum*, where the passion for cleaning was indulged without control. In this sacred apartment no one was permitted to enter, excepting the mistress and her confidential maid, who visited it once a week, for the purpose of giving it a thorough cleaning, and putting things to rights—always taking the precaution of leaving their shoes at the door, and entering devoutly in their stocking-feet. After scrubbing the floor, sprinkling it with fine white sand, which was curiously stroked into angles, and curves, and rhomboids,¹ with a broom—after washing the windows, rubbing and polishing the furniture, and putting a new bunch of evergreens in the fire-place—the window-shutters were again closed to keep out the flies, and the room carefully locked up until the revolution of time brought round the weekly cleaning day.

As to the family, they always entered in at the gate, and most generally lived in the kitchen. To have seen a numerous household assembled around the fire, one would have imagined that he was transported back to those happy days of primeval simplicity, which float before our imaginations like golden visions. The fire-places were of a truly patriarchal magnitude, where the whole family, old and young, master and servant, black and white, nay, even the very cat and dog, enjoyed a community of privilege, and had each a right to a corner. Here the old burgher would sit in perfect silence, puffing his pipe, looking in the fire with half-shut eyes, and thinking of nothing for hours together ; the goede vrouw ² on

---

¹ a non-equilateral oblique parallelogram, such as might easily be made by a series of straight lines crossing each other.   ² good wife.

the opposite side would employ herself diligently in spinning yarn, or knitting stockings. The young folks would crowd around the hearth, listening with breathless attention to some old crone of a negro, who was the oracle of the family, and who, perched like a raven in the corner of the chimney, would croak forth for a long winter afternoon a string of incredible stories about New-England witches [1]—grisly ghosts, horses without heads—and hairbreadth escapes and bloody encounters among the Indians.

In those happy days a well-regulated family always rose with the dawn, dined at eleven, and went to bed at sun-down. Dinner was invariably a private meal, and the fat old burghers showed incontestable symptoms of disapprobation and uneasiness at being surprised by a visit from a neighbor on such occasions. But though our worthy ancestors were thus singularly averse to giving dinners, yet they kept up the social bands of intimacy by occasional banquetings, called tea-parties.

These fashionable parties were generally confined to the higher classes, or noblesse, that is to say, such as kept their own cows, and drove their own wagons. The company commonly assembled at three o'clock, and went away about six, unless it was in winter-time, when the fashionable hours were a little earlier, that the ladies might get home before dark. The tea-table was crowned with a huge earthen dish, well stored with slices of fat pork, fried brown, cut up into morsels, and swimming in gravy. The company being seated around the genial board, and each furnished with a fork, evinced their dexterity in launching at the fattest pieces in this mighty dish—in much the same manner as sailors harpoon porpoises at sea, or our Indians spear salmon in the lakes. Sometimes the table was graced with immense apple pies, or saucers full of preserved peaches and pears; but it was always

---

[1] The belief in witches still continued in the seventeenth century. In New England the superstition grew at one time into a fever of excitement, in the course of which many poor creatures were unjustly put to death. Irving often refers to New England witches. See pp. 62, 84, 113.

sure to boast an enormous dish of balls of sweetened dough, fried in hog's fat, and called doughnuts, or olykoeks—a delicious kind of cake, at present scarce known in this city, excepting in genuine Dutch families.

The tea was served out of a majestic Delft tea-pot, ornamented with paintings of fat little Dutch shepherds and shepherdesses tending pigs—with boats sailing in the air, and houses built in the clouds, and sundry other ingenious Dutch fantasies. The beaux distinguished themselves by their adroitness in replenishing this pot from a huge copper tea-kettle, which would have made the pigmy macaronics[1] of these degenerate days sweat merely to look at it. To sweeten the beverage, a lump of sugar was laid beside each cup—and the company alternately nibbled and sipped with great decorum, until an improvement was introduced by a shrewd and economic old lady, which was to suspend a large lump directly over the tea-table, by a string from the ceiling, so that it could be swung from mouth to mouth—an ingenious expedient which is still kept up by some families in Albany ; but which prevails without exception in Communipaw, Bergen, Flatbush, and all our uncontaminated Dutch villages.

At these primitive tea-parties the utmost propriety and dignity of deportment prevailed. No flirting nor coquetting—no gambling of old ladies, nor hoyden chattering and romping of young ones—no self-satisfied struttings of wealthy gentlemen, with their brains in their pockets—nor amusing conceits, and monkey divertisements, of smart young gentlemen with no brains at all. On the contrary, the young ladies seated themselves demurely in their rush-bottomed chairs, and knit their own woollen stockings ; nor ever opened their lips, excepting to say, *yah Mynheer*, or *yah ya Vrouw*,[2] to any question that was asked them ; behaving, in all things, like decent, well-educated damsels. As to the gentlemen, each of them tran-

[1] a name current in Irving's day for dandies. Cf. " Yankee Doodle."
[2] Yes, sir. Yes, madam.

quilly smoked his pipe, and seemed lost in contemplation of the blue and white tiles with which the fire-places were decorated ; wherein sundry passages of Scripture were piously portrayed— Tobit [1] and his dog figured to great advantage ; Haman [2] swung conspicuously on his gibbet ; and Jonah [3] appeared most manfully bouncing out of the whale, like Harlequin through a barrel of fire.

The parties broke up without noise and without confusion. They were carried home by their own carriages, that is to say, by the vehicles Nature had provided them, excepting such of the wealthy as could afford to keep a wagon. The gentlemen gallantly attended their fair ones to their respective abodes, and took leave of them with a hearty smack at the door; which, as it was an established piece of etiquette, done in perfect simplicity and honesty of heart, occasioned no scandal at that time, nor should it at the present—if our great-grandfathers approved of the custom, it would argue a great want of reverence in their descendants to say a word against it.

In this dulcet period of my history, when the beauteous island of Manna-hata [4] presented a scene, the very counterpart of those glowing pictures drawn of the golden reign of Saturn, [5] there was, as I have before observed, a happy ignorance, an honest simplicity, prevalent among its inhabitants, which, were I even able to depict, would be but little understood by the degenerate age for which I am doomed to write. Even the female sex, those arch innovators upon the tranquillity, the honesty, and gray-beard customs of society, seemed for a while to conduct themselves with incredible sobriety and comeliness.

[1] The Book of Tobit alludes twice to Tobit's dog (iv. 16, xi. 4).

[2] Esther vii. 10.   [3] Jonah ii. 10.

[4] The Indian name for the island on which the city of New Amsterdam was built is now generally spelled Manhattan. In the seventeenth century, however, there were various other spellings as well. Irving has both Manhattoes and Manna-hata, as here.

[5] one of the ancient gods, whose reign was of the utmost peace and harmony.

Their hair, untortured by the abominations of art, was scrupulously pomatumed back from their foreheads with a candle, and covered with a little cap of quilted calico, which fitted exactly to their heads.   Their petticoats of linsey-woolsey were striped with a variety of gorgeous dyes—though I must confess these gallant garments were rather short, scarce reaching below the knee ; but then they made up in the number, which generally equalled that of the gentlemen's small-clothes ;[1] and what is still more praiseworthy, they were all of their own manufacture—of which circumstance, as may well be supposed, they were not a little vain.

These were the honest days, in which every woman staid at home, read the Bible, and wore pockets—ay, and that too of a goodly size, fashioned with patchwork into many curious devices, and ostentatiously worn on the outside.   These, in fact, were convenient receptacles, where all good housewives carefully stowed away such things as they wished to have at hand ; by which means they often came to be incredibly crammed—and I remember there was a story current when I was a boy, that the lady of Wouter Van Twiller once had occasion to empty her right pocket in search of a wooden ladle, and the utensil was discovered lying among some rubbish in one corner—but we must not give too much faith to all these stories ; the anecdotes of those remote periods being very subject to exaggeration.

Besides these notable pockets, they likewise wore scissors and pincushions suspended from their girdles by red ribands, or, among the more opulent and showy classes, by brass, and even silver chains, indubitable tokens of thrifty housewives and industrious spinsters.   I cannot say much in vindication of the shortness of the petticoats ; it doubtless was introduced for the purpose of giving the stockings a chance to be seen, which were generally of blue worsted, with magnificent red clocks—or perhaps to display a well-turned ankle, and a neat,

---

[1] knee-breeches.

though serviceable, foot, set off by a high-heeled leathern shoe with a large and splendid silver buckle. Thus we find that the gentle sex in all ages have shown the same disposition to infringe a little upon the laws of decorum, in order to betray a lurking beauty, or gratify an innocent love of finery.

From the sketch here given, it will be seen that our good grandmothers differed considerably in their ideas of a fine figure from their scantily-dressed descendants of the present day. A fine lady, in those times, waddled under more clothes, even on a fair summer's day, than would have clad the whole bevy of a modern ball-room. Nor were they the less admired by the gentlemen in consequence thereof. On the contrary, the greatness of a lover's passion seemed to increase in proportion to the magnitude of its object—and a voluminous damsel, arrayed in a dozen of petticoats, was declared by a Low Dutch sonnetteer[1] of the province to be as radiant as a sun-flower, and luxuriant as a full-blown cabbage. Certain it is, that in those days, the heart of a lover could not contain more than one lady at a time ; whereas the heart of a modern gallant has often room enough to accommodate half-a-dozen. The reason of which I conclude to be, that either the hearts of the gentlemen have grown larger, or the persons of the ladies smaller—this, however, is a question for physiologists to determine.

But there was a secret charm in these petticoats, which no doubt entered into the consideration of the prudent gallants. The wardrobe of a lady was in those days her only fortune ; and she who had a good stock of petticoats and stockings was as absolutely an heiress as is a Kamtschatka damsel with a store of bear-skins, or a Lapland belle with a plenty of rein-deer. The ladies, therefore, were very anxious to display these powerful attractions to the greatest advantage ; and the best rooms in the house, instead of being adorned with carica-

---

[1] A sonnet is a particular kind of short poem. Here, however, Irving merely means a writer of love-poetry.

tures of dame Nature, in water-colors and needle-work, were always hung round with abundance of home-spun garments, the manufacture and the property of the females—a piece of laudable ostentation that still prevails among the heiresses of our Dutch villages.

The gentlemen, in fact, who figured in the circles of the gay world in these ancient times, corresponded, in most particulars, with the beauteous damsels whose smiles they were ambitious to deserve. True it is, their merits would make but a very inconsiderable impression upon the heart of a modern fair ; they neither drove their curricles nor sported their tandems, for as yet those gaudy vehicles were not even dreamt of—neither did they distinguish themselves by their brilliancy at the table and their consequent rencontres[1] with watchmen,[2] for our forefathers were of too pacific a disposition to need those guardians of the night, every soul throughout the town being sound asleep before nine o'clock. Neither did they establish their claims to gentility at the expense of their tailors—for as yet those offenders against the pockets of society and the tranquillity of all aspiring young gentlemen were unknown in New-Amsterdam ; every good housewife made the clothes of her husband and family, and even the goede vrouw of Van Twiller himself thought it no disparagement to cut out her husband's linsey-woolsey galligaskins.[3]

Not but what there were some two or three youngsters who manifested the first dawning of what is called fire and spirit —who held all labor in contempt ; skulked about docks and market-places ; loitered in the sunshine ; squandered what little money they could procure at hustle-cap and chuck-farthing ; swore, boxed, fought cocks, and raced their neighbors'

[1] a French word, now not much used in English, meaning a sudden meeting.

[2] Before the establishment of a regular police force, watchmen patrolled the streets at night.

[3] a kind of loose, short trousers worn in the sixteenth century. Such trousers are meant here; elsewhere (p. 89) Irving merely uses the word in a general way.

horses—in short, who promised to be the wonder, the talk, and abomination of the town, had not their stylish career been unfortunately cut short by an affair of honor with a whipping-post.

Far other, however, was the truly fashionable gentleman of those days—his dress, which served for both morning and evening, street and drawing-room, was a linsey-woolsey coat, made, perhaps, by the fair hands of the mistress of his affections, and gallantly bedecked with abundance of large brass buttons—half a score of breeches heightened the proportions of his figure—his shoes were decorated by enormous copper buckles—a low-crowned, broad-brimmed hat overshadowed his burly visage, and his hair dangled down his back in a prodigious queue of eel-skin.

Thus equipped, he would manfully sally forth with pipe in mouth, to besiege some fair damsel's obdurate heart—not such a pipe,[1] good reader, as that which Acis did sweetly tune in praise of his Galatea,[2] but one of true Delft[3] manufacture, and furnished with a charge of fragrant tobacco. With this would he resolutely set himself down before the fortress, and rarely failed, in the process of time, to smoke the fair enemy into a surrender, upon honorable terms.

Such was the happy reign of Wouter Van Twiller, celebrated in many a long-forgotten song as the real golden age, the rest being nothing but counterfeit copper-washed coin. In that delightful period a sweet and holy calm reigned over the whole province. The burgomaster smoked his pipe in peace—the substantial solace of his domestic cares, after her daily toils were done, sat soberly at the door, with her arms crossed over her apron of snowy white, without being insulted by ribald street-walkers, or vagabond boys—those unlucky urchins, who

---

[1] formerly a musical instrument.
[2] Galatea, a Sicilian maiden, loved by Acis. He was, however, slain by Polyphemus, a jealous rival.

[3] originally the name of a place in Holland, famous for its potteries. The pipes Irving had in mind were the porcelain pipes common in Holland and Germany.

do so infest our streets, displaying under the roses of youth the thorns and briars of iniquity.

Ah ! blissful, and never-to-be-forgotten age ! when every thing was better than it has ever been since, or ever will be again—when Buttermilk Channel was quite dry at low water —when the shad in the Hudson were all salmon, and when the moon shone with a pure and resplendent whiteness, instead of that melancholy yellow light which is the consequence of her sickening at the abominations she every night witnesses in this degenerate city !

Happy would it have been for New-Amsterdam, could it always have existed in this state of blissful ignorance and lowly simplicity—but, alas ! the days of childhood are too sweet to last ! Cities, like men, grow out of them in time, and are doomed alike to grow into the bustle, the cares, and miseries of the world. Let no man congratulate himself when he beholds the child of his bosom or the city of his birth increasing in magnitude and importance—let the history of his own life teach him the dangers of the one, and this excellent little history of Manna-hata convince him of the calamities of the other.[1]

---

[1] It should, perhaps, be pointed out that in this description of New York, Irving is transferring to the time of Van Twiller things which were true only of a later day. Van Twiller was Director from 1633 to 1637. During all his time New Amsterdam was but a small trading-post. " Population had increased but slowly," says Roosevelt, "and the town which huddled round the fort on the south point of Manhattan Island was little more than a collection of poor hovels." The streets, the houses with brick gables, the comfortable farmers, the burgomasters, belong to a later period—perhaps to the latter part of the rule of Stuyvesant, about twenty-five years afterward.

II *b.*—HOW WILLIAM THE TESTY DE-
FENDED THE CITY.

AS DESCRIBED IN KNICKERBOCKER'S HISTORY OF NEW YORK, BOOK IV., CHAPTER IV.[1]

LANGUAGE cannot express the prodigious fury into which the testy Wilhelmus Kieft was thrown by this provoking intelligence.[2] For three good hours the rage of the little man was too great for words, or rather the words were too great for him ; and he was nearly choked by some dozen huge, mis-shapen, nine-cornered Dutch oaths, that crowded all at once into his gullet. Having blazed off the first broadside, he kept up a constant firing for three whole days—anathematizing the Yankees, man, woman, and child, body and soul, for a set of dieven, schobbejaken, deugenieten, twist-zoekeren, loozen-schalken, blaes-kaken, kakken-bedden,[3] and a thousand other names, of which, unfortunately for posterity, history does not make mention. Finally, he swore that he would have nothing more to do with such a squatting, bundling, guessing, ques-tioning, swapping, pumpkin-eating, molasses-daubing, shingle-splitting, cider-watering, horse-jockeying, notion-peddling crew—that they might stay at Fort Good Hoop and rot, before he would dirty his hands by attempting to drive them away ; in proof of which, he ordered the new-raised[4] troops to be marched forthwith into winter-quarters, although it was not as yet quite mid-summer. Governor Kieft faithfully kept his word, and his adversaries as faithfully kept their post ; and thus the glorious river Connecticut, and all the gay valleys through which it rolls, together with the salmon, shad, and

---

[1] The later editions of "Knickerbocker" present this matter in more extended form.

[2] namely, the news that the New England-ers had dispossessed the Dutch of Fort Good Hope on the Connecticut River. See p. 14.

[3] "thieves, rogues, good - for - nothings, quarrel-breeders, crafty fellows, boasters."

[4] Kieft had been raising a force to go against the Yankees.

other fish within its waters, fell into the hands of the victorious Yankees, by whom they are held at this very day.

Great despondency seized upon the city of New-Amsterdam, in consequence of these melancholy events. The name of Yankee became as terrible among our good ancestors as was that of Gaul[1] among the ancient Romans; and all the sage old women of the province used it as a bugbear, wherewith to frighten their unruly children into obedience.

The eyes of all the province were now turned upon their governor, to know what he would do for the protection of the common weal,[2] in these days of darkness and peril. Great apprehensions prevailed among the reflecting part of the community, especially the old women, that these terrible warriors of Connecticut, not content with the conquest of Fort Good Hoop, would incontinently march on to New-Amsterdam and take it by storm—and as these old ladies, through means of the governor's spouse, who, as has been already hinted, was "the better horse,"[3] had obtained considerable influence in public affairs, keeping the province under a kind of petticoat government, it was determined that measures should be taken for the effective fortification of the city.

Now it happened, that at this time there sojourned in New-Amsterdam one Antony Van Corlear, a jolly fat Dutch trumpeter, of a pleasant burly visage, famous for his long wind and his huge whiskers, and who, as the story goes, could twang so potently upon his instrument, as to produce an effect upon all within hearing, as though ten thousand bag-pipes were singing right lustily i' the nose. Him did the illustrious Kieft pick out as the man of all the world most fitted to be the champion of New-Amsterdam, and to garrison its fort; making little doubt but that his instrument would be as effec-

---

[1] the ancient name for what is now France.

[2] or commonwealth: the two terms are often found in older English, meaning "the state."

[3] In a previous chapter Irving told how Kieft was much under the domination of his wife. Irving, as a bachelor, has here a conventionally humorous view of marriage, as in "Rip Van Winkle."

tual and offensive in war as was that of the paladin Astolpho,[1] or the more classic horn of Alecto.[2]   It would have done one's heart good to have seen the governor snapping his fingers and fidgeting with delight, while his sturdy trumpeter strutted up and down the ramparts, fearlessly twanging his trumpet in the face of the whole world, like a thrice-valorous editor daringly insulting all the principalities and powers—on the other side of the Atlantic.

Nor was he content with thus strongly garrisoning the fort, but he likewise added exceedingly to its strength by furnishing it with a formidable battery of quaker guns[3]—rearing a stupendous flag-staff in the centre, which overtopped the whole city—and, moreover, by building a great windmill on one of the bastions.[4]   This last, to be sure, was somewhat of a novelty in the art of fortification, but, as I have already observed, William Kieft was notorious for innovations and experiments ; and traditions do affirm, that he was much given to mechanical inventions — constructing patent smoke-jacks[5]—carts that went before the horses, and especially erecting windmills, for which machines he had acquired a singular predilection in his native town of Saardam.[6]

All these scientific vagaries of the little governor were cried up with ecstasy by his adherents, as proofs of his universal genius—but there were not wanting ill-natured grumblers, who railed at him as employing his mind in frivolous pursuits, and devoting that time to smoke-jacks and windmills which should have been occupied in the more important concerns of the province.   Nay, they even went so far as to hint, once or twice,

[1] The paladins were the chief knights of Charlemagne, very famous in romance. Astolpho had a magic horn which put to flight all who heard it.

[2] Alecto was one of the Furies in ancient mythology.

[3] a slang term for imitation cannon made of wood, the Quakers being unwarlike in character.

[4] the angle of a fortification, generally strongly fortified.

[5] A smoke-jack is a machine set in the chimney for turning a roasting-spit.

[6] a town of Holland, not far from Amsterdam. It is famous for the four hundred windmills said to be here and there in the neighborhood.

that his head was turned by his experiments, and that he really thought to manage his government as he did his mills—by mere wind!—such are the illiberality and slander to which enlightened rulers are ever subject.

Notwithstanding all the measures, therefore, of William the Testy, to place the city in a posture of defence, the inhabitants continued in great alarm and despondency. But fortune, who seems always careful, in the very nick of time, to throw a bone for hope to gnaw upon, that the starveling elf may be kept alive, did about this time crown the arms of the province with success in another quarter, and thus cheered the drooping hearts of the forlorn Nederlanders; otherwise, there is no knowing to what lengths they might have gone in the excess of their sorrowing—"for grief," says the profound historian of the seven champions of Christendom,[1] "is companion with despair, and despair a procurer of infamous death!"

Among the numerous inroads of the mosstroopers[2] of Connecticut, which for some time past had occasioned such great tribulation, I should particularly have mentioned a settlement made on the eastern part of Long Island, at a place which, from the peculiar excellence of its shell-fish, was called Oyster Bay.[3] This was attacking the province in the most sensible[4] part, and occasioned great agitation at New-Amsterdam.

It is an incontrovertible fact, well known to skilful physiologists, that the high road to the affections is through the throat; and this may be accounted for on the same principles which I have already quoted in my strictures on fat aldermen. Nor is the fact unknown to the world at large; and hence do we observe, that the surest way to gain the hearts of the million,

[1] "The Seven Champions of Christendom" was a famous old story-book.

[2] the name given, in old times, to the Scotch borderers, as in "The Lay of the Last Minstrel."

[3] Long Island, although claimed by the Dutch, was settled in part by the New England landers, who also laid claim to the whole island. They did not succeed in establishing their claim, but when New Amsterdam was threatened, and finally taken by an English fleet (p. 15), these Long Islanders were on hand to assist their countrymen.

[4] susceptible to feeling.

is to feed them well—and that a man is never so disposed to
flatter, to please and serve another, as when he is feeding at
his expense ; which is one reason why your rich men, who give
frequent dinners, have such abundance of sincere and faithful
friends.   It is on this principle that our knowing leaders of
parties secure the affections of their partisans, by rewarding
them bountifully with loaves and fishes ; and entrap the suf-
frages of the greasy mob, by treating them with bull feasts and
roasted oxen.   I have known many a man, in this same city,
acquire considerable importance in society, and usurp a large
share of the good-will of his enlightened fellow-citizens, when
the only thing that could be said in his eulogium was, that
" he gave a good dinner, and kept excellent wine."

Since, then, the heart and the stomach are so nearly allied,
it follows conclusively that what affects the one, must sympa-
thetically affect the other.   Now, it is an equally incontrovertible fact, that of all offerings to the stomach, there is none
more grateful than the testaceous marine animal, known commonly by the vulgar name of Oyster.   And in such great reverence has it ever been held, by my gormandizing fellow-citizens, that temples have been dedicated to it, time out of mind,
in every street, lane, and alley throughout this well-fed city.
It is not to be expected, therefore, that the seizing of Oyster
Bay, a place abounding with their favorite delicacy, would be
tolerated by the inhabitants of New-Amsterdam.   An attack
upon their honor they might have pardoned ; even the mas-
sacre of a few citizens might have been passed over in silence ;
but an outrage that affected the larders of the great city of
New-Amsterdam, and threatened the stomachs of its corpulent
burgomasters, was too serious to pass unrevenged.—The whole
council was unanimous in opinion, that the intruders should
be immediately driven by force of arms from Oyster Bay and
its vicinity, and a detachment was accordingly despatched for
the purpose, under the command of one Stoffel Brinkerhoff,
or Brinkerhoofd, (*i.e.* Stoffel, the head-breaker,) so called be-

cause he was a man of mighty deeds, famous throughout the whole extent of Nieuw-Nederlandts for his skill at quarter-staff ;[1] and for size, he would have been a match for Colbrand, the Danish champion, slain by Guy of Warwick.[2]

Stoffel Brinkerhoff was a man of few words, but prompt actions—one of your straight-going officers, who march directly forward ; and do their orders without making any parade. He used no extraordinary speed in his movements, but trudged steadily on, through Nineveh and Babylon, and Jericho and Patchog, and the mighty town of Quag, and various other renowned cities of yore, which, by some unaccountable witchcraft of the Yankees, have been strangely transplanted to Long Island, until he arrived in the neighborhood of Oyster Bay.

Here was he encountered by a tumultuous host of valiant warriors, headed by Preserved [3] Fish, and Habakkuk Nutter, and Return Strong, and Zerubbabel Fish, and Jonathan Doolittle, and Determined Cock !—at the sound of whose names the courageous Stoffel verily believed that the whole parliament of Praise-God Barebones [4] had been let loose to discomfit him.   Finding, however, that this formidable body was composed merely of the " select men " [5] of the settlement, armed with no other weapons but their tongues, and that they had issued forth with no other intent than to meet him on the field of argument,—he succeeded in putting them to the rout with little difficulty, and completely broke up their settlement. Without waiting to write an account of his victory on the

<hr>

[1] a long staff, used formerly as a weapon of offence and defence. It was held in the middle, so that both ends could be used to strike and parry with.

[2] a legendary figure of English romance. His battle with Colbrand was supposed to have been in the days of Athelstan, when the Danes and Anglo-Saxons were constantly at war in England.

[3] These curious Christian names were

not invented by Irving. The Puritans had many such strange names, often taken from the Bible.

[4] Praisegod Barebones was a real character. He was a member of the English Parliament of 1653, which was called, in derision, "Barebones' Parliament."

[5] the title of the governing body of a New England village.

4

spot, and thus letting the enemy slip through his fingers, while
he was securing his own laurels, as a more experienced general
would have done, the brave Stoffel thought of nothing but
completing his enterprise, and utterly driving the Yankees
from the island.   This hardy enterprise he performed in much
the same manner as he had been accustomed to drive his oxen ;
for as the Yankees fled before him, he pulled up his breeches
and trudged steadily after them, and would infallibly have
driven them into the sea, had they not begged for quarter, and
agreed to pay tribute.[1]

The news of this achievement was a seasonable restorative
to the spirits of the citizens of New-Amsterdam.   To gratify
them still more, the governor resolved to astonish them with
one of those gorgeous spectacles known in the days of classic
antiquity, a full account of which had been flogged into his
memory, when a school-boy at the Hague.   A grand triumph,
therefore, was decreed to Stoffel Brinkerhoff, who made his triumphant entrance into town riding on a Narraganset pacer ;[2]
five pumpkins, which, like Roman eagles, had served the
enemy for standards, were carried before him—fifty cart loads
of oysters, five hundred bushels of Weathersfield onions, a hundred quintals of codfish, two hogsheads of molasses, and various other treasures, were exhibited as the spoils and tribute of
the Yankees ; while three notorious counterfeiters of Manhattan notes were led captive, to grace the hero's triumph.   The
procession was enlivened by martial music from the trumpet
of Antony Van Corlear, the champion, accompanied by a
select band of boys and negroes performing on the national
instruments of rattle-bones and clam-shells.   The citizens de-
voured the spoils in sheer gladness of heart—every man did
honor to the conqueror, by getting devoutly drunk on New-
England rum—and the learned Wilhelmus Kieft, calling to

---

[1] The Dutch maintained their claim to Long Island, which is the reason that it is now a part of New York.

[2] The horses from the Narragansett country in Rhode Island were well known in the beginning of the century. They seem to have been commonly trained to pace.

mind, in a momentary fit of enthusiasm and generosity, that it was customary among the ancients to honor their victorious generals with public statues, passed a gracious decree, by which every tavern-keeper was permitted to paint the head of the intrepid Stoffel on his sign !

II c.—PETER STUYVESANT'S VOYAGE UP THE HUDSON.

AS DESCRIBED IN KNICKERBOCKER'S HISTORY OF NEW YORK, BOOK VI., CHAPTER IV.

Now did the soft breezes of the south steal sweetly over the beauteous face of nature, tempering the panting heats of summer into genial and prolific warmth ; when that miracle of hardihood and chivalric virtue, the dauntless Peter Stuyvesant,[1] spread his canvas to the wind, and departed from the fair island of Manna-hata.   The galley[2] in which he embarked was sumptuously adorned with pendants and streamers of gorgeous dyes, which fluttered gayly in the wind, or drooped their ends in the bosom of the stream.   The bow and poop of this majestic vessel were gallantly bedight, after the rarest Dutch fashion, with figures of little pursy Cupids with periwigs[3] on their heads, and bearing in their hands garlands of flowers, the like of which are not to be found in any book of botany ; being the matchless flowers which flourished in the golden age, and exist no longer, unless it be in the imaginations of ingenious carvers of wood and discolorers of canvas.

Thus rarely decorated, in style befitting the state of the puissant potentate of the Manhattoes, did the galley of Peter Stuyvesant launch forth upon the bosom of the lordly Hudson ;

---

[1] the fourth and last Director of New Amsterdam under the Dutch. He was a man of great determination ; Irving calls him Peter the Headstrong.

[2] in this case, only a poetic word for "vessel."

[3] a corruption, through the Dutch, of French *perruque*, a wig.

which, as it rolled its broad waves to the ocean, seemed to pause for a while, and swell with pride, as if conscious of the illustrious burthen it sustained.

But trust me, gentlefolk, far other was the scene presented to the contemplation of the crew, from that which may be witnessed at this degenerate day. Wildness and savage majesty reigned on the borders of this mighty river—the hand of cultivation had not as yet laid down the dark forests, and tamed the features of the landscape—nor had the frequent sail of commerce yet broken in upon the profound and awful solitude of ages. Here and there might be seen a rude wigwam perched among the cliffs of the mountains, with its curling column of smoke mounting in the transparent atmosphere—but so loftily situated, that the whooping of the savage children, gambolling on the margin of the dizzy heights, fell almost as faintly on the ear as do the notes of the lark when lost in the azure vault of heaven. Now and then, from the beetling brow of some rocky precipice, the wild deer would look timidly down upon the splendid pageant as it passed below ; and then, tossing his branching antlers in the air, would bound away into the thickest of the forest.

Through such scenes did the stately vessel of Peter Stuyvesant pass. Now did they skirt the bases of the rocky heights of Jersey,[1] which spring up like everlasting walls, reaching from the waves unto the heavens ; and were fashioned, if traditions may be believed, in times long past, by the mighty spirit Manetho, to protect his favorite abodes from the unhallowed eyes of mortals. Now did they career it gayly across the vast expanse of Tappan Bay,[2] whose wide extended shores present a vast variety of delectable scenery—here the bold promontory, crowned with embowering trees, advancing into the bay— there the long woodland slope, sweeping up from the shore in rich luxuriance, and terminating in the upland precipice— while at a distance a long waving line of rocky heights threw ·

---

[1] the Palisades.   [2] Irving generally calls it Tappaan Zee, as on p. 58.

their gigantic shades across the water.   Now would they pass
where some modest little interval, opening among these stupendous scenes, yet retreating as it were for protection into the
embraces of the neighboring mountains, displayed a rural
paradise, fraught with sweet and pastoral beauties ; the velvet-
tufted lawn—the bushy copse—the tinkling rivulet, stealing
through the fresh and vivid verdure—on whose banks was
situated some little Indian village, or, peradventure, the rude
cabin of some solitary hunter.

The different periods of the revolving day seemed each, with
cunning magic, to diffuse a different charm over the scene.
Now would the jovial sun break gloriously from the east, blaz-
ing from the summits of the hills, and sparkling the landscape
with a thousand dewy gems ; while along the borders of the
river were seen heavy masses of mist, which, like midnight
caitiffs, disturbed at his approach, made a sluggish retreat,
rolling in sullen reluctance up the mountains.   At such times,
all was brightness and life and gayety—the atmosphere seemed
of an indescribable pureness and transparency—the birds
broke forth in wanton madrigals, and the freshening breezes
wafted the vessel merrily on her course.   But when the sun
sunk amid a flood of glory in the west, mantling the heavens
and the earth with a thousand gorgeous dyes—then all was
calm, and silent, and magnificent.   The late swelling sail hung
lifelessly against the mast—the seaman with folded arms leaned
against the shrouds, lost in that involuntary musing which the
sober grandeur of nature commands in the rudest of her children.   The vast bosom of the Hudson was like an unruffled
mirror, reflecting the golden splendor of the heavens, excepting that now and then a bark canoe would steal across its surface, filled with painted savages, whose gay feathers glared
brightly, as perchance a lingering ray of the setting sun
gleamed upon them from the western mountains.

But when the hour of twilight spread its magic mists around,
then did the face of nature assume a thousand fugitive charms,

which, to the worthy heart that seeks enjoyment in the glorious works of its Maker, are inexpressibly captivating. The mellow dubious light that prevailed, just served to tinge with illusive colors the softened features of the scenery. The deceived but delighted eye sought vainly to discern, in the broad masses of shade, the separating line between the land and water; or to distinguish the fading objects that seemed sinking into chaos. Now did the busy fancy supply the feebleness of vision, producing with industrious craft a fairy creation of her own. Under her plastic wand the barren rocks frowned upon the watery waste, in the semblance of lofty towers and high embattled castles—trees assumed the direful forms of mighty giants, and the inaccessible summits of the mountains seemed peopled with a thousand shadowy beings.

Now broke forth from the shores the notes of an innumerable variety of insects, which filled the air with a strange but not inharmonious concert—while ever and anon was heard the melancholy plaint of the whip-poor-will, who, perched on some lone tree, wearied the ear of night with his incessant moanings. The mind, soothed into a hallowed melancholy, listened with pensive stillness to catch and distinguish each sound that vaguely echoed from the shore—now and then startled perchance by the whoop of some straggling savage, or the dreary howl of a wolf, stealing forth upon his nightly prowlings.

Thus happily did they pursue their course, until they entered upon those awful defiles denominated THE HIGHLANDS, where it would seem that the gigantic Titans[1] had erst waged their impious war with heaven, piling up cliffs on cliffs, and hurling vast masses of rock in wild confusion. But in sooth, very different is the history of these cloud-capped mountains.—These in ancient days, before the Hudson poured his waters from the lakes, formed one vast prison, within whose rocky bosom the omnipotent Manetho confined the rebellious spirits who repined at his control. Here, bound in adamantine chains, or jammed

[1] gigantic beings of the Greek mythology, who warred with the gods.

in rifted pines, or crushed by ponderous rocks, they groaned
for many an age.   At length the conquering Hudson, in his
irresistible career towards the ocean, burst open their prison-
house, rolling his tide triumphantly through its stupendous
ruins.

Still, however, do many of them lurk about their old abodes ;
and these it is, according to venerable legends, that cause the
echoes which resound throughout these awful solitudes ; which
are nothing but their angry clamors, when any noise disturbs
the profoundness of their repose.   For when the elements are
agitated by tempest, when the winds are up and the thunder
rolls, then horrible is the yelling and howling of these troubled
spirits, making the mountains to rebellow with their hideous
uproar ; for at such times, it is said, they think the great
Manetho is returning once more to plunge them in gloomy
caverns, and renew their intolerable captivity.

But all these fair and glorious scenes were lost upon the gallant Stuyvesant ; nought occupied his mind but thoughts of
iron war, and proud anticipations of hardy deeds of arms.
Neither did his honest crew trouble their vacant heads with
any romantic speculations of the kind.   The pilot at the helm
quietly smoked his pipe, thinking of nothing either past, present, or to come—those of his comrades who were not indus-
triously snoring under the hatches were listening with open
mouths to Antony Van Corlear ; who, seated on the windlass,
was relating to them the marvellous history of those myriads
of fire-flies that sparkled like gems and spangles upon the
dusky robe of night.   These, according to tradition, were
originally a race of pestilent sempiternous beldames, who peopled these parts long before the memory of man ; being of that
abominated race emphatically called *brimstones ;* and who, for
their innumerable sins against the children of men, and to
furnish an awful warning to the beauteous sex, were doomed
to infest the earth in the shape of these threatening and terrible little bugs ; enduring the internal torments of that fire,

which they formerly carried in their hearts, and breathed
forth in their words ; but now are sentenced to bear about for
ever—in their tails.

And now I am going to tell a fact, which I doubt much my
readers will hesitate to believe ; but if they do, they are welcome not to believe a word in this whole history, for nothing
which it contains is more true.   It must be known then that
the nose of Antony the trumpeter was of a very lusty size,
strutting boldly from his countenance like a mountain of Golconda ;[1] being sumptuously bedecked with rubies and other
precious stones—the true regalia of a king of good fellows,
which jolly Bacchus[2] grants to all who bouse it heartily at the
flagon.   Now thus it happened, that bright and early in the
morning, the good Antony having washed his burly visage,
was leaning over the quarter-railing of the galley contemplat-
ing it in the glassy wave below—just at this moment, the
illustrious sun, breaking in all his splendor from behind one
of the high bluffs of the Highlands, did dart one of his most
potent beams full upon the refulgent nose of the sounder of
brass—the reflection of which shot straightway down, hissing
hot, into the water, and killed a mighty sturgeon that was
sporting beside the vessel !   This huge monster being with
infinite labor hoisted on board, furnished a luxurious repast to
all the crew, being accounted of excellent flavor, excepting
about the wound, where it smacked a little of brimstone—and
this, on my veracity, was the first time that ever sturgeon was
eaten in these parts by Christian people.[*]

When this astonishing miracle came to be made known to
Peter Stuyvesant, and that he tasted of the unknown fish, he,
as may well be supposed, marvelled exceedingly ; and as a
monument thereof, he gave the name *Antony's Nose* to a

---

[1] the diamond mines of Golconda, near
Hyderabad, India.

[2] the Roman god of wine.

[*] The learned Hans Megapolensis, treating of the country about Albany, in a letter
which was written some time after the settlement thereof, says : "There is in the
river great plenty of Sturgeon, which we
Christians do not make use of ; but the Indians eat them greedilie."—*Author's Note.*

stout promontory in the neighborhood—and it has continued to be called Antony's Nose[1] ever since that time.

But hold—Whither am I wandering?—By the mass, if I attempt to accompany the good Peter Stuyvesant on this voyage, I shall never make an end, for never was there a voyage so fraught with marvellous incidents, nor a river so abounding with transcendent beauties, worthy of being severally recorded. Even now I have it on the point of my pen to relate, how his crew were most horribly frightened, on going on shore above the Highlands, by a gang of merry, roistering devils, frisking and curveting on a huge flat rock, which projected into the river—and which is called the *Duyvel's Dans-Kamer*[2] to this very day.—But no! Diedrich Knickerbocker—it becomes thee not to idle thus in thy historic wayfaring.

Recollect that while dwelling with the fond garrulity of age over these fairy scenes, endeared to thee by the recollections of thy youth, and the charms of a thousand legendary tales which beguiled the simple ear of thy childhood; recollect that thou art trifling with those fleeting moments which should be devoted to loftier themes.—Is not Time—relentless Time!—shaking, with palsied hand, his almost exhausted hour-glass before thee?—hasten then to pursue thy weary task, lest the last sands be run, ere thou hast finished thy history of the Manhattoes.

Let us then commit the dauntless Peter, his brave galley, and his loyal crew, to the protection of the blessed St. Nicholas; who, I have no doubt, will prosper him in his voyage, while we await his return at the great city of New-Amsterdam.[3]

[1] See map, p. 10.

[2] Devil's Dance-hall.

[3] Irving's first journey up the Hudson was made in the year 1800, when he was seventeen years of age. He went to Albany in a sloop, and in this account of Stuyvesant's voyage there is doubtless much remembrance of that early trip. "What a time of intense delight," he writes, "was that first sail through the Highlands! I sat on the deck as we slowly tided along at the foot of those stern mountains, and gazed with wonder and admiration at cliffs impending far above me, crowned with forests, with eagles sailing and screaming around them; or listened to the unseen stream dashing down precipices; or beheld rock, and tree, and cloud, and sky reflected in the glassy stream of the river. And then how solemn and thrilling the scene

III.—WOLFERT'S ROOST.

CHRONICLE I.

About five-and-twenty miles from the ancient and renowned city of Manhattan,[1] formerly called New-Amsterdam, and vulgarly[2] called New-York, on the eastern bank of that expansion of the Hudson, known among Dutch mariners of yore, as the Tappaan Zee,[3] being in fact the great Mediterranean Sea[4] of the New-Netherlands,[5] stands a little old-fashioned stone mansion,[6] all made up of gable ends, and as full of angles and corners as an old cocked hat. It is said, in fact, to have been modelled after the cocked hat of Peter the Headstrong,[7] as the Escurial[8] was modelled after the gridiron of the blessed St. Lawrence. Though but of small dimensions, yet, like many small people, it is of mighty spirit, and values itself greatly on its antiquity, being one of the oldest edifices, for its size, in the whole country. It claims to be an ancient seat of empire, I may rather say an empire in itself, and like all empires, great and small, has had its grand historical epochs. In speaking of this doughty and valorous little pile,[9] I shall call it by its usual appellation of "The Roost;" though that is a name given to it in modern days, since it became the abode of the white man.

Its origin, in truth, dates far back in that remote region commonly called the fabulous age, in which vulgar fact

---

as we anchored at night at the foot of these mountains, clothed with overhanging forests; and everything grew dark and mysterious; and I heard the plaintive note of the whip-poor-will from the mountain-side, or was startled now and then by the sudden leap and heavy splash of the sturgeon."— *Life and Letters*, i., 19.

[1] See p. 38, note.   [2] commonly.

[3] The name "Tappaan" appears on very early maps, as applied to the expansion of the Hudson south of Croton Point.

[4] The name means "in the middle of the world."

[5] the name of the Dutch possessions in America.

[6] See Introduction, p. 17.

[7] Peter Stuyvesant (p. 13).

[8] the royal palace at Madrid; a reminiscence of Irving's years in Spain.

[9] a term often applied to great buildings; here somewhat humorous. Irving's cottage, "The Roost," was afterward, as has been said (p. 18), called "Sunnyside."

becomes mystified, and tinted up with delectable fiction. The
eastern shore of the Tappan Sea was inhabited in those days
by an unsophisticated race, existing in all the simplicity of
nature ; that is to say, they lived by hunting and fishing, and
recreated themselves occasionally with a little tomahawking
and scalping. Each stream that flows down from the hills
into the Hudson, had its petty sachem, who ruled over a
hand's breadth of forest on either side, and had his seat of
government at its mouth. The chieftain who ruled at the
Roost, was not merely a great warrior, but a medicine-man,
or prophet, or conjurer, for they all mean the same thing in
Indian parlance. Of his fighting propensities, evidences still
remain, in various arrow-heads of flint, and stone battle-axes,
occasionally digged up about the Roost : of his wizard powers,
we have a token in a spring which wells up at the foot of the
bank, on the very margin of the river, which, it is said, was
gifted by him with rejuvenating powers, something like the
renowned Fountain of Youth[1] in the Floridas, so anxiously
but vainly sought after by the veteran Ponce de Leon.[2] This
story, however, is stoutly contradicted by an old Dutch matter-
of-fact tradition, which declares that the spring in question
was smuggled over from Holland in a churn, by Femmetie
Van Blarcom, wife of Goosen Garret Van Blarcom, one of the
first settlers, and that she took it up by night, unknown to
her husband, from beside their farm-house near Rotterdam ;
being sure she should find no water equal to it in the new
country—and she was right.

The wizard sachem had a great passion for discussing territo-
rial questions, and settling boundary lines, in other words, he
had the spirit of annexation ; this kept him in continual feud
with the neighboring sachems, each of whom stood up stoutly
for his hand-breadth of territory ; so that there is not a petty

[1] The Fountain of Youth, whose waters
made one young again, was eagerly sought
by the Spaniards.

[2] the discoverer of Florida. He was
killed in a fight with the Indians in 1501, on
an expedition in search of the fabled island
of Bimini, in which was the famous fountain.

stream nor rugged hill in the neighborhood, that has not been the subject of long talks and hard battles. The sachem, however, as has been observed, was a medicine-man, as well as warrior, and vindicated his claims by arts as well as arms; so that, by dint of a little hard fighting here, and hocus pocus (or diplomacy) there, he managed to extend his boundary line from field to field and stream to stream, until it brought him into collision with the powerful sachem of Sing-Sing. Many were the sharp conflicts between these rival chieftains for the sovereignty of a winding valley, a favorite hunting ground watered by a beautiful stream called the Pocantico. Many were the ambuscades, surprisals, and deadly onslaughts that took place among its fastnesses, of which it grieves me much that I cannot pursue the details, for the gratification of those gentle but bloody-minded readers, of both sexes, who delight in the romance of the tomahawk and scalping-knife. Suffice it to say, that the wizard chieftain was at length victorious, though his victory is attributed, in Indian tradition, to a great medicine, or charm, by which he laid the sachem of Sing-Sing and his warriors asleep among the rocks and recesses of the valley, where they remain asleep to the present day, with their bows and war-clubs beside them.[1] This was the origin of that potent and drowsy spell, which still prevails over the valley of the Pocantico, and which has gained it the well-merited appellation of Sleepy Hollow. Often, in secluded and quiet parts of that valley, where the stream is overhung by dark woods and rocks, the ploughman, on some calm and sunny day, as he shouts to his oxen, is surprised at hearing faint shouts from the hill-sides in reply; being, it is said, the spell-bound warriors, who half start from their rocky couches and grasp their weapons, but sink to sleep again.

The conquest of the Pocantico was the last triumph of the

[1] The same legend is current in Germany, where the great emperor Frederick Barbarossa sleeps with all his men, some say in the vaults of his old palace of Kaiserslautern, some say in the castle of Rodenstein, some under the Kyffhäuser.

wizard sachem. Notwithstanding all his medicines and charms, he fell in battle, in attempting to extend his boundary line to the east, so as to take in the little wild valley of the Sprain, and his grave is still shown, near the banks of that pastoral stream. He left, however, a great empire to his successors, extending along the Tappan Sea, from Yonkers quite to Sleepy Hollow, and known in old records and maps by the Indian name of Wicquaes-Keck.[1]

The wizard sachem was succeeded by a line of chiefs of whom nothing remarkable remains on record. One of them was the very individual on whom master Hendrick Hudson[2] and his mate Robert Juet[3] made that sage experiment gravely recorded by the latter, in the narrative of the discovery.

" Our master and his mate determined to try some of the cheefe men of the country, whether they had any treacherie in them. So they took them down into the cabin, and gave them so much wine and aqua vitæ, that they were all very merrie; one of them had his wife with him, which sate so modestly as any of our countrywomen would do in a strange place. In the end, one of them was drunke; and that was strange to them, for they could not tell how to take it."[*]

How far master Hendrick Hudson and his worthy mate carried their experiment with the sachem's wife, is not recorded, neither does the curious Robert Juet make any mention of the after consequences of this grand moral test; tradition, however, affirms that the sachem, on landing, gave his modest spouse a hearty rib-roasting, according to the connubial discipline of the aboriginals; it farther affirms, that he remained a hard drinker to the day of his death, trading away all his lands, acre by acre, for aqua vitæ; by which means the Roost and all its domains, from Yonkers to Sleepy Hollow, came, in the regular course of trade, and by right of purchase, into the possession of the Dutchmen.

---

[1] This name may be found on Van der Donck's map (1656).

[2] See p. 12.

[3] one of Hudson's sailors, who kept a journal.

[*] See Juet's Journal, Purchas' Pilgrims.

The worthy government of the New Netherlands was not suffered to enjoy this grand acquisition unmolested. In the year 1654, the losel [1] Yankees of Connecticut, those swapping, bargaining, squatting enemies of the Manhattoes, made a daring inroad into this neighborhood, and founded a colony called Westchester, [2] or, as the ancient Dutch records term it, Vest Dorp, in the right of one Thomas Pell, who pretended to have purchased the whole surrounding country of the Indians; and stood ready to argue their claims before any tribunal of Christendom.

This happened during the chivalrous reign of Peter Stuyvesant, and roused the ire of that gunpowder old hero. Without waiting to discuss claims and titles, he pounced at once upon the nest of nefarious squatters, carried off twenty-five of them in chains to the Manhattoes, nor did he stay his hand, nor give rest to his wooden leg, until he had driven the rest of the Yankees back into Connecticut, or obliged them to acknowledge allegiance to their High Mightinesses. In revenge, however, they introduced the plague of witchcraft [3] into the province. This doleful malady broke out at Vest Dorp, and would have spread throughout the country had not the Dutch farmers nailed horse-shoes to the doors of their houses and barns, sure protections against witchcraft, many of which remain to the present day.

The seat of empire of the wizard sachem now came into the possession of Wolfert Acker, one of the privy counsellors of Peter Stuyvesant. He was a worthy, but ill-starred man, whose aim through life had been to live in peace and quiet. For this he had emigrated from Holland, driven abroad by family feuds and wrangling neighbors. He had warred for quiet through the fidgetting reign of William the Testy, [4] and the fighting reign of Peter the Headstrong, [5] sharing in every brawl and

---

[1] worthless, wasteful.
[2] now the name of the county. The word has the same meaning as Vest Dorp.

[3] See p. 36, note 1.
[4] William Kieft, the third Director.
[5] See p. 51, note 1.

rib-roasting, in his eagerness to keep the peace and promote public tranquillity. It was his doom, in fact, to meet a head wind at every turn, and be kept in a constant fume and fret by the perverseness of mankind. Had he served on a modern jury he would have been sure to have eleven unreasonable men opposed to him.

At the time [1] when the province of the New Netherlands was wrested from the domination of their High Mightinesses [2] by the combined forces of Old and New England, Wolfert retired in high dudgeon to this fastness in the wilderness, with the bitter determination to bury himself from the world, and live here for the rest of his days in peace and quiet. In token of that fixed purpose he inscribed over his door (his teeth clenched at the time) his favorite Dutch motto, " Lust in Rust," (pleasure in quiet). The mansion was thence called Wolfert's Rust—(Wolfert's Rest), but by the uneducated, who did not understand Dutch, Wolfert's Roost ; probably from its quaint cock-loft look, and from its having a weather-cock perched on every gable.

Wolfert's luck followed him into retirement. He had shut himself up from the world, but he had brought with him a wife, and it soon passed into a proverb throughout the neighborhood that the cock of the Roost was the most henpecked bird in the country. His house too was reputed to be harassed by Yankee witchcraft. When the weather was quiet everywhere else, the wind, it was said, would howl and whistle about the gables ; witches and warlocks would whirl about upon the weather-cocks and scream down the chimneys ; nay, it was even hinted that Wolfert's wife was in league with the enemy, and used to ride on a broomstick to a witches' sabbath in Sleepy Hollow. This, however, was all mere scandal, founded perhaps on her occasionally flourishing a broomstick in the course of a curtain lecture, or raising a storm within doors,

[1] namely, in 1664.
[2] the title of the rulers of the United Provinces.

as termagant wives are apt to do, and against which sorcery horse-shoes are of no avail.

Wolfert Acker died and was buried, but found no quiet even in the grave: for if popular gossip be true, his ghost has occasionally been seen walking by moonlight among the old gray moss-grown trees of his apple orchard.

CHRONICLE II.

The next period at which we find this venerable and eventful pile rising into importance, was during the dark and troublous time of the revolutionary war. It was the keep or stronghold of Jacob Van Tassel, a valiant Dutchman of the old stock of Van Tassels,[1] who abound in Westchester County. The name, as originally written, was Van Texel, being derived from the Texel[2] in Holland, which gave birth to that heroic line.

The Roost stood in the very heart of what at that time was called the debatable ground,[3] lying between the British and American lines. The British held possession of the city and island of New York; while the Americans drew up towards the Highlands, holding their head-quarters at Peekskill. The intervening country from Croton River to Spiting Devil Creek was the debatable ground in question, liable to be harried by friend and foe, like the Scottish borders of yore.[4]

It is a rugged region; full of fastnesses. A line of rocky hills extends through it like a backbone, sending out ribs on either side; but these rude hills are for the most part richly wooded, and inclose little fresh pastoral valleys watered by the Neperan, the Pocantico,* and other beautiful streams, along which the Indians built their wigwams in the olden time.

[1] One of them, in after years, was Baltus Van Tassel of Sleepy Hollow, who had a daughter Katrina, as we shall learn later.

[2] an island on the coast of Holland.

[3] often used as a proper name, Debatable Ground.

[4] See the "Lay of the Last Minstrel."

* The Neperan, vulgarly called the Saw-Mill River, winds for many miles through a lovely valley, shrouded by groves, and dotted by Dutch farm-houses, and empties itself into the Hudson, at the ancient Dorp of Yonkers. The Pocantico, rising among woody hills, winds in many a wizard maze, through the sequestered haunts of Sleepy Hollow. We owe it to the indefatigable

In the fastnesses of these hills, and along these valleys existed, in the time of which I am treating, and indeed exist to the present day, a race of hard-headed, hard-handed, stout-hearted yeomanry descendants of the primitive Nederlanders. Men obstinately attached to the soil, and neither to be fought nor bought out of their paternal acres. Most of them were strong Whigs [1] throughout the war; some, however, were Tories, [1] or adherents to the old kingly rule; who considered the revolution a mere rebellion, soon to be put down by his majesty's forces. A number of these took refuge within the British lines, joined the military bands of refugees, and became pioneers or leaders to foraging parties sent out from New York to scour the country and sweep off supplies for the British army.

In a little while the debatable ground became infested by roving bands, claiming from either side, and all pretending to redress wrongs and punish political offences; but all prone in the exercise of their high functions, to sack hen-roosts, drive off cattle, and lay farm-houses under contribution: such was the origin of two great orders of border chivalry, the Skinners and the Cow Boys, [2] famous in revolutionary story; the former fought, or rather marauded under the American, the latter under the British banner. In the zeal of service, both were apt to make blunders, and confound the property of friend and foe. Neither of them in the heat and hurry of a foray had time to ascertain the politics of a horse or cow, which they were driving off into captivity; nor, when they wrung the neck of a rooster, did they trouble their heads whether he crowed for Congress or King George.

To check these enormities, a confederacy was formed among

researches of Mr. KNICKERBOCKER, that those beautiful streams are rescued from modern common-place, and reinvested with their ancient Indian names. The correctness of the venerable historian may be ascertained by reference to the records of the original Indian grants to Herr Frederick Philipsen, preserved in the county clerk's office, at White Plains.—*Author's note.*

[1] Whigs was the name given to the patriots in the Revolution, Tories to those who espoused the cause of the British.

[2] Cf. Cooper's novel, "The Spy."

5

the yeomanry who had suffered from these maraudings. It
was composed for the most part of farmers' sons, bold, hard-
riding lads, well armed, and well mounted, and undertook to
clear the country round of Skinner, and Cow Boy, and all
other border vermin ; as the Holy Brotherhood [1] in old times
cleared Spain of the banditti which infested her highways.

Wolfert's Roost was one of the rallying places of this confederacy, and Jacob Van Tassel one of its members. He was
eminently fitted for the service : stout of frame, bold of heart,
and like his predecessor, the warrior sachem of yore, delighting in daring enterprises. He had an Indian's sagacity in
discovering when the enemy was on the maraud, and in hearing the distant tramp of cattle. It seemed as if he had a
scout on every hill, and an ear as quick as that of Fine Ear
in the fairy tale.

The foraging parties of tories and refugees had now to be
secret and sudden in their forays into Westchester County ; to
make a hasty maraud among the farms, sweep the cattle into
a drove, and hurry down to the lines along the river road, or
the valley of the Neperan. Before they were half way down,
Jacob Van Tassel, with the holy brotherhood of Tarrytown,
Petticoat Lane, and Sleepy Hollow, would be clattering at
their heels. And now there would be a general scamper for
King's Bridge, the pass over Spiting Devil Creek into the
British lines. Sometimes the moss-troopers [2] would be overtaken, and eased of part of their booty. Sometimes the whole
cavalgada [3] would urge its headlong course across the bridge
with thundering tramp and dusty whirlwind. At such times
their pursuers would rein up their steeds, survey that perilous
pass with wary eye and, wheeling about, indemnify themselves
by foraging the refugee region of Morrisania. [4]

While the debatable land was liable to be thus harried, the

[1] The reference to Spain comes from Irving's long familiarity with that country.

[2] the name given to the Scotch border ers alluded to.

[3] more like Spanish than English ; the correct form would be *cabalgada*.

[4] a former village of Westchester ; now a part of New York.

great Tappan Sea, along which it extends, was likewise domineered over by the foe. British ships of war were anchored here and there in the wide expanses of the river, mere floating castles[1] to hold it in subjection. Stout galleys armed with eighteen pounders, and navigated with sails and oars, cruised about like hawks; while row-boats made descents upon the land, and foraged the country along shore.

It was a sore grievance to the yeomanry along the Tappan Sea to behold that little Mediterranean ploughed by hostile prows, and the noble river of which they were so proud, reduced to a state of thraldom. Councils of war were held by captains of market-boats and other river craft, to devise ways and means of dislodging the enemy. Here and there on a point of land extending into the Tappan Sea, a mud-work would be thrown up, and an old field-piece mounted, with which a knot of rustic artillerymen would fire away for a long summer's day at some frigate dozing at anchor far out of reach : and reliques of such works may still be seen overgrown with weeds and brambles, with peradventure the half-buried fragment of a cannon which may have burst.

Jacob Van Tassel was a prominent man in these belligerent operations ; but he was prone moreover, to carry on a petty warfare of his own for his individual recreation and refreshment. On a row of hooks above the fireplace of the Roost, reposed his great piece of ordnance ; a duck, or rather goose gun of unparalleled longitude, with which it was said he could kill a wild goose half way across the Tappan Sea. Indeed there are as many wonders told of this renowned gun, as of the enchanted weapons of classic story. When the belligerent feeling was strong upon Jacob, he would take down his gun, sally forth alone, and prowl along shore, dodging behind rocks and trees, watching for hours together any ship or galley at anchor or becalmed ; as a valorous mouser will watch a rat

---

[1] *i.e.*, they remained in one place while the galleys and rowboats flew about. A galley is a good-sized vessel propelled by oars.

hole. So sure as a boat approached the shore, bang ! went the great goose-gun, sending on board a shower of slugs and buck shot ; and away scuttled Jacob Van Tassel through some woody ravine. As the Roost stood in a lonely situation, and might be attacked, he guarded against surprise by making loop-holes in the stone walls, through which to fire upon an assailant. His wife was stout-hearted as himself, and could load as fast as he could fire, and his sister, Nochie Van Wurmer, a redoubtable widow, was a match, as he said, for the stoutest man in the country. Thus garrisoned, his little castle was fitted to stand a siege, and Jacob was the man to defend it to the last charge of powder.

In the process of time the Roost became one of the secret stations, or lurking places, of the Water Guard. This was an aquatic corps in the pay of government, organized to range the waters of the Hudson, and keep watch upon the movements of the enemy. It was composed of nautical men of the river and hardy youngsters of the adjacent country, expert at pulling an oar or handling a musket. They were provided with whale-boats, long and sharp, shaped like canoes, and formed to lie lightly on the water, and be rowed with great rapidity. In these they would lurk out of sight by day, in nooks and bays, and behind points of land ; keeping a sharp look-out upon the British ships, and giving intelligence to head-quarters of any extraordinary movement. At night they rowed about in pairs, pulling quietly along with muffled oars, under shadow of the land, or gliding like spectres about frigates and guard ships to cut off any boat that might be sent to shore. In this way they were a source of constant uneasiness and alarm to the enemy.

The Roost, as has been observed, was one of their lurking places ; having a cove in front where their whale-boats could be drawn up out of sight, and Jacob Van Tassel being a vigilant ally ready to take a part in any "scout or scrummage" . by land or water. At this little warrior nest the hard-riding

lads from the hills would hold consultations with the chivalry
of the river, and here were concerted divers of those daring
enterprises[1] which resounded from Spiting Devil Creek even
unto Anthony's Nose. Here was concocted the midnight
invasion of New York Island, and the conflagration of De-
lancy's Tory mansion, which makes such a blaze in revolutionary history. Nay more, if the traditions of the Roost
may be credited, here was meditated by Jacob Van Tassel and
his compeers, a nocturnal foray into New York itself, to surprise and carry off the British commanders Howe[2] and Clinton,[3] and put a triumphant close to the war.

There is no knowing whether this notable scheme might
not have been carried into effect, had not one of Jacob Van
Tassel's egregious exploits along shore with his goose-gun,
with which he thought himself a match for any thing, brought
vengeance on his house.

It so happened, that in the course of one of his solitary
prowls he descried a British transport[4] aground; the stern
swung toward shore within point-blank shot. The temptation
was too great to be resisted. Bang! went the great goose-
gun, from the covert of the trees, shivering the cabin windows
and driving all hands forward. Bang! bang! the shots were
repeated. The reports brought other of Jacob's fellow bush-
fighters to the spot. Before the transport could bring a gun
to bear, or land a boat to take revenge, she was soundly pep-
pered, and the coast evacuated.

This was the last of Jacob's triumphs. He fared like some
heroic spider that has unwittingly ensnared a hornet to the
utter ruin of his web. It was not long after the above exploit
that he fell into the hands of the enemy in the course of one
of his forays, and was carried away prisoner to New York.
The Roost itself, as a pestilent rebel nest, was marked out for

---

[1] New York was in British hands from
Sept. 5, 1776, till Nov. 25, 1783. Various
unsuccessful attempts were made by the
Americans to get the city out of their hands.

[2] Richard, Lord Howe, was English commander-in-chief in America, 1776-1778.

[3] Sir Henry Clinton succeeded Howe.

[4] a vessel used for carrying soldiers.

signal punishment. The cock of the Roost being captive, there was none to garrison it but his stout-hearted spouse, his redoubtable sister, Nochie Van Wurmer, and Dinah, a strapping negro wench. An armed vessel came to anchor in front ; a boat full of men pulled to shore. The garrison flew to arms ; that is to say, to mops, broomsticks, shovels, tongs, and all kinds of domestic weapons ; for unluckily, the great piece of ordnance, the goose-gun, was absent with its owner. Above all, a vigorous defence was made with the most potent of female weapons, the tongue. Never did invaded hen-roost make a more vociferous outcry. It was all in vain. The house was sacked and plundered, fire was set to each corner, and in a few moments its blaze shed a baleful light far over the Tappan Sea. The invaders then pounced upon the blooming Laney Van Tassel, the beauty of the Roost, and endeavored to bear her off to the boat. But here was the real tug of war. The mother, the aunt, and the strapping negro wench, all flew to the rescue. The struggle continued down to the very water's edge ; when a voice from the armed vessel at anchor, ordered the spoilers to desist ; they relinquished their prize, jumped into their boats, and pulled off, and the heroine of the Roost escaped with a mere rumpling of the feathers.

As to the stout Jacob himself, he was detained a prisoner in New York for the greater part of the war ; in the mean time the Roost remained a melancholy ruin, its stone walls and brick chimneys alone standing, the resorts of bats and owls. Superstitious notions prevailed about it. None of the country people would venture alone at night down the rambling lane which led to it, overhung with trees and crossed here and there by a wild wandering brook. The story went that one of the victims of Jacob Van Tassel's great goose-gun had been buried there in unconsecrated ground.

Even the Tappan Sea in front was said to be haunted. Often in the still twilight of a summer evening, when the Sea would be as glass, and the opposite hills would throw their purple

shadows half across it, a low sound would be heard as of the
steady vigorous pull of oars, though not a boat was to be
descried. Some might have supposed that a boat was rowed
along unseen under the deep shadows of the opposite shores;
but the ancient traditionists of the neighborhood knew better.
Some said it was one of the whale-boats of the old water-guard,
sunk by the British ships during the war, but now permitted
to haunt its old cruising grounds; but the prevalent opinion connected it with the awful fate of Rambout Van Dam
of graceless memory. He was a roystering Dutchman of Spiting Devil, who in times long past had navigated his boat alone
one Saturday the whole length of the Tappan Sea, to attend
a quilting frolic at Kakiat, on the western shore. Here he had
danced, and drunk, until midnight, when he entered his boat
to return home. He was warned that he was on the verge of
Sunday morning; but he pulled off nevertheless, swearing he
would not land until he reached Spiting Devil, if it took him
a month of Sundays. He was never seen afterwards; but
may be heard plying his oars, as above mentioned, being the
Flying Dutchman [1] of the Tappan Sea, doomed to ply between
Kakiat and Spiting Devil until the day of judgment.

CHRONICLE III.

The revolutionary war was over. The debatable ground
had once more become a quiet agricultural region; the border
chivalry had turned their swords into ploughshares, and their
spears into pruning hooks, and hung up their guns, only
to be taken down occasionally in a campaign against wild
pigeons on the hills, or wild ducks upon the Hudson. Jacob
Van Tassel, whilome [2] carried captive to New York, a flagi-
tious rebel, had come forth from captivity a " hero of seventy-

---

[1] The legend of the Flying Dutchman is
of Vanderdecken, a Dutch sea captain, who
failed in his effort to double the Cape of
Good Hope. He swore blasphemously that
he would double the cape in spite of God

himself, and was condemned to expiate his
offence by eternal sailing to and fro on the
ocean until the last day, being allowed to
land but once in seven years.

[2] formerly.

six." In a little while he sought the scenes of his former
triumphs and mishaps, rebuilt the Roost, restored his goose-
gun to the hooks over the fireplace, and reared once more on
high the glittering weathercocks.

Years and years passed over the time-honored little mansion. The honeysuckle and the sweetbrier crept up its walls ;
the wren and the phœbe bird built under the eaves ; it
gradually became almost hidden among trees, through which
it looked forth, as with half-shut eyes, upon the Tappan Sea.
The Indian spring, famous in the days of the wizard sachem,
still welled up at the bottom of the green bank ; and the wild
brook, wild as ever, came babbling down the ravine, and threw
itself into the little cove where of yore the water-guard har-
bored their whaleboats.

Such was the state of the Roost many years since, at the
time when Diedrich Knickerbocker [1] came into this neighborhood, in the course of his researches among the Dutch families for materials for his immortal history. The exterior of
the eventful little pile seemed to him full of promise. The
crow-step gables were of the primitive architecture of the
province. The weathercocks which surmounted them had
crowed in the glorious days of the New-Netherlands. The
one above the porch had actually glittered of yore on the
great Vander Heyden palace at Albany !

The interior of the mansion fulfilled its external promise.
Here were records of old times ; documents of the Dutch
dynasty, rescued from the profane hands of the English, by
Wolfert Acker, when he retreated from New Amsterdam.
Here he had treasured them up like buried gold, and here
they had been miraculously preserved by St. Nicholas, [2] at the
time of the conflagration of the Roost.

Here then did old Diedrich Knickerbocker take up his abode
for a time, and set to work with antiquarian zeal to decipher
these precious documents, which, like the lost books of

---

[1] See Introduction, p. 16.   [2] patron saint of the New Netherlands.

Livy,[1] had baffled the research of former historians; and it is the facts drawn from these sources which give his work the preference, in point of accuracy, over every other history.

It was during his sojourn in this eventful neighborhood, that the historian is supposed to have picked up many of those legends, which have since been given by him to the world, or found among his papers. Such was the legend connected with the old Dutch church of Sleepy Hollow. The church itself was a monument of bygone days. It had been built in the early times of the province. A tablet over the portal bore the names of its founders: Frederick Filipson, a mighty man of yore, patroon of Yonkers, and his wife Katrina Van Courtland, of the Van Courtlands of Croton; a powerful family connexion, with one foot resting on Spiting Devil Creek, and the other on the Croton River.

Two weathercocks, with the initials of these illustrious personages, graced each end of the church, one perched over the belfry, the other over the chancel. As usual with ecclesiastical weathercocks, each pointed a different way; and there was a perpetual contradiction between them on all points of windy doctrine; emblematic, alas! of the Christian propensity to schism and controversy.

In the burying-ground adjacent to the church, reposed the earliest fathers of a wide rural neighborhood. Here families were garnered together, side by side, in long platoons, in this last gathering place of kindred. With pious hand would Diedrich Knickerbocker turn down the weeds and brambles which had overgrown the tombstones, to decipher inscriptions in Dutch and English, of the names and virtues of succeeding generations of Van Tassels, Van Warts, and other historical worthies, with their portraitures faithfully carved, all bearing the family likeness to cherubs.

The congregation in those days was of a truly rural character. City fashions had not as yet stole up to Sleepy Hollow.

[1] The complete text of Livy's "History of Rome" has never been recovered.

Dutch sun-bonnets and honest homespun still prevailed. Every thing was in primitive style, even to the bucket of water and tin cup near the door in summer, to assuage the thirst caused by the heat of the weather or the drouth of the sermon.

The pulpit, with its wide-spreading sounding board, and the communion table, curiously carved, had each come from Holland in the olden time, before the arts had sufficiently advanced in the colony for such achievements. Around these on Sundays would be gathered the elders of the church, grayheaded men who led the psalmody, and in whom it would be difficult to recognize the hard-riding lads of yore, who scoured the debatable land in the time of the Revolution.

The drowsy influence of Sleepy Hollow was apt to breathe into this sacred edifice ; and now and then an elder might be seen with his handkerchief over his face to keep off the flies, and apparently listening to the dominie ; but really sunk into a summer slumber, lulled by the sultry notes of the locust from the neighboring trees.

And now a word or two about Sleepy Hollow, which many have rashly deemed a fanciful creation, like the Lubberland [1] of mariners. It was probably the mystic and dreamy sound of the name which first tempted the historian of the Manhattoes into its spellbound mazes. As he entered, all nature seemed for the moment to awake from its slumbers and break forth in gratulations. The quail whistled a welcome from the corn field ; the loquacious cat-bird flew from bush to bush with restless wing proclaiming his approach, or perked inquisitively into his face, as if to get a knowledge of his physiognomy. The woodpecker tapped a tattoo on the hollow apple tree, and then peered round the trunk, as if asking how he relished the salutation ; while the squirrel scampered along the fence, whisking his tail over his head by way of a huzza.

[1] a name sometimes given to a fancied land where there was nothing to do and plenty to eat and drink.

Here reigned the golden mean [1] extolled by poets, in which no gold was to be found and very little silver. The inhabitants of the Hollow were of the primitive stock, and had intermarried and bred in and in, from the earliest time of the province, never swarming far from the parent hive, but dividing and subdividing their paternal acres as they swarmed.

Here were small farms, each having its little portion of meadow and corn field ; its orchard of gnarled and sprawling apple trees ; its garden in which the rose, the marigold and hollyhock, grew sociably with the cabbage, the pea, and the pumpkin : each had its low-eaved mansion redundant [2] with white-headed children ; with an old hat nailed against the wall for the housekeeping wren ; the coop on the grass-plot, where the motherly hen clucked round with her vagrant brood : each had its stone well, with a moss-covered bucket suspended to the long balancing pole, according to antediluvian hydraulics ; [3] while within doors resounded the eternal hum of the spinning wheel.

Many were the great historical facts which the worthy Diedrich collected in these lowly mansions, and patiently would he sit by the old Dutch housewives with a child on his knee, or a purring grimalkin on his lap, listing to endless ghost stories spun forth to the humming accompaniment of the wheel.

The delighted historian pursued his explorations far into the foldings of the hills where the Pocantico winds its wizard stream among the mazes of its old Indian haunts ; sometimes running darkly in pieces of woodland beneath balancing sprays of beech and chestnut : sometimes sparkling between grassy borders in fresh green intervals ; here and there receiving the tributes of silver rills which came whimpering down the hill-sides from their parent springs.

In a remote part of the Hollow, where the Pocantico forced its way down rugged rocks, stood Carl's mill, the haunted

[1] the right point between too much and too little. [2] having more than is necessary. [3] "antediluvian," before the flood ; "hydraulics," water-works.

house of the neighborhood. It was indeed a goblin-looking
pile ; shattered and time-worn ; dismal with clanking wheels
and rushing streams, and all kinds of uncouth noises. A
horse-shoe nailed to the door to keep off witches, seemed to
have lost its power ; for as Diedrich approached, an old negro
thrust his head all dabbled with flour, out of a hole above the
water wheel, and grinned and rolled his eyes, and appeared to
be the very hobgoblin of the place. Yet this proved to be the
great historic genius of the Hollow, abounding in that valuable information never to be acquired from books. Diedrich
Knickerbocker soon discovered his merit. They had long
talks together seated on a broken millstone, heedless of the
water and the clatter of the mill ; and to his conference with
that African sage, many attribute the surprising, though true
story of Ichabod Crane,[1] and the Headless Horseman of Sleepy
Hollow. We refrain, however, from giving farther researches
of the historian of the Manhattoes, during his sojourn at the
Roost ; but may return to them in future pages.

Reader, the Roost still exists. Time, which changes all
things, is slow in its operations on a Dutchman's dwelling.
The stout Jacob Van Tassel, it is true, sleeps with his fathers ;
and his great goose-gun with him : yet his stronghold still
bears the impress of its Dutch origin. Odd rumors have
gathered about it, as they are apt to do about old mansions,
like moss and weather stains. The shade of Wolfert Acker
still walks his unquiet rounds at night in the orchard ; and a
white figure has now and then been seen seated at a window
and gazing at the moon, from a room in which a young lady
is said to have died of love and green apples.

Mementoes of the sojourn of Diedrich Knickerbocker are
still cherished at the Roost. His elbow chair and antique
writing-desk maintain their place in the room he occupied,
and his old cocked hat still hangs on a peg against the wall.

---

[1] the story originally told in the "Sketch Book," which was published many years
before " Wolfert's Roost."

IV.—THE STORM-SHIP.

IN the golden age [1] of the province of the New-Nether-lands, when it was under the sway of Wouter Van Twiller,[2] otherwise called the Doubter,[3] the people of the Manhattoes[4] were alarmed, one sultry afternoon, just about the time of the summer solstice,[5] by a tremendous storm of thunder and light-ning. The rain descended in such torrents, as absolutely to spatter up and smoke along the ground. It seemed as if the thunder rattled and rolled over the very roofs of the houses; the lightning was seen to play about the church of St. Nicho-las, and to strive three times, in vain, to strike its weather-cock. Garret Van Horne's new chimney was split almost from top to bottom; and Doffue Mildeberger was struck speechless from his bald-faced mare, just as he was riding into town. In a word, it was one of those unparalleled storms, that only happen once within the memory of that venerable personage, known in all towns by the appellation of "the oldest inhabitant."

Great was the terror of the good old women of the Manhat-toes. They gathered their children together, and took refuge in the cellars; after having hung a shoe on the iron point of every bed-post, lest it should attract the lightning. At length the storm abated; the thunder sunk into a growl; and the setting sun, breaking from under the fringed borders of the clouds, made the broad bosom of the bay to gleam like a sea of molten gold.[6]

The word was given from the fort, that a ship was standing up the bay. It passed from mouth to mouth, and street to

---

[1] Irving always speaks of the time of Van Twiller in this way. See pp. 33, 38.

[2] the second Director, 1633-1637. See p. 41.

[3] by Irving himself in " Knickerbocker."

[4] one of the early forms of Manhattan (p. 38, note).

[5] The summer solstice comes on June 21st.

[6] This touch of nature may be verified by any one who has the fortune to have the sea to the west of him in the summer.

street, and soon put the little capital in a bustle. The arrival
of a ship, in those early times of the settlement, was an event
of vast importance to the inhabitants. It brought them news
from the old world, from the land of their birth, from which
they were so completely severed : to the yearly ship,[1] too, they
looked for their supply of luxuries, of finery, of comforts, and
almost of necessaries. The good vrouw[2] could not have her
new cap, nor new gown, until the arrival of the ship ; the artist
waited for it for his tools, the burgomaster for his pipe and his
supply of Hollands, the school-boy for his top and marbles,
and the lordly landholder for the bricks[3] with which he was to
build his new mansion. Thus every one, rich and poor, great
and small, looked out for the arrival of the ship. It was the
great yearly event of the town of New-Amsterdam ; and from
one end of the year to the other, the ship—the ship—the ship
—was the continual topic of conversation.

The news from the fort, therefore, brought all the populace
down to the battery,[4] to behold the wished-for sight. It was
not exactly the time when she had been expected to arrive,
and the circumstance was a matter of some speculation. Many
were the groups collected about the battery. Here and there
might be seen a burgomaster,[5] of slow and pompous gravity,
giving his opinion with great confidence to a crowd of old
women and idle boys. At another place was a knot of old
weatherbeaten fellows, who had been seamen or fishermen in
their times, and were great authorities on such occasions ; these
gave different opinions, and caused great disputes among their
several adherents : but the man most looked up to, and followed and watched by the crowd, was Hans Van Pelt, an old
Dutch sea-captain retired from service, the nautical oracle

---

[1] the yearly ship sent out by the company
at home.

[2] Dutch for " woman " or " wife " ; the
German form is *frau*.

[3] Bricks were not yet made in the new
country, although now very many brick-
kilns may be seen on the Hudson.

[4] The Battery still exists as a name in
New York.

[5] Strictly speaking, there were no burgomasters in New York till 1653, when finally,
under Stuyvesant, New Amsterdam was
incorporated as a city. The burgomasters
were members of the legislative council.

of the place. He reconnoitred the ship through an ancient telescope, covered with tarry canvas, hummed a Dutch tune to himself, and said nothing. A hum, however, from Hans Van Pelt had always more weight with the public than a speech from another man.

In the meantime, the ship became more distinct to the naked eye : she was a stout, round Dutch-built vessel, with high bow and poop, and bearing Dutch colors. The evening sun gilded her bellying canvas, as she came riding over the long waving billows. The sentinel who had given notice of her approach, declared, that he first got sight of her when she was in the centre of the bay ; and that she broke suddenly on his sight, just as if she had come out of the bosom of the black thunder-cloud. The bystanders looked at Hans Van Pelt, to see what he would say to this report : Hans Van Pelt screwed his mouth closer together, and said nothing ; upon which some shook their heads, and others shrugged their shoulders.

The ship was now repeatedly hailed, but made no reply, and, passing by the fort, stood on up the Hudson. A gun was brought to bear on her,[1] and, with some difficulty, loaded and fired by Hans Van Pelt, the garrison not being expert in artillery. The shot seemed absolutely to pass through the ship, and to skip along the water on the other side, but no notice was taken of it ! What was strange, she had all her sails set, and sailed right against wind and tide, which were both down the river. Upon this Hans Van Pelt, who was likewise harbor-master, ordered his boat, and set off to board her ; but after rowing two or three hours, he returned without success. Sometimes he would get within one or two hundred yards of her, and then, in a twinkling, she would be half a mile off. Some said it was because his oarsmen, who were rather pursy and short-winded, stopped every now and then to take breath, and spit on their hands ; but this, it is probable, was a mere scandal. He got near enough, however, to see the crew ; who

---

[1] A shot fired over the bows of a ship is a sign that she must come to.

were all dressed in the Dutch style, the officers in doublets and high hats and feathers : not a word was spoken by any one on board ; they stood as motionless as so many statues, and the ship seemed as if left to her own government. Thus she kept on, away up the river, lessening and lessening in the evening sunshine, until she faded from sight, like a little white cloud melting away in the summer sky.

The appearance of this ship threw the governor into one of the deepest doubts[1] that ever beset him in the whole course of his administration. Fears were entertained for the security of the infant settlements on the river, lest this might be an enemy's ship in disguise, sent to take possession. The governor called together his council repeatedly to assist him with their conjectures. He sat in his chair of state, built of timber from the sacred forest of the Hague, and smoking his long jasmine pipe, and listened to all that his counsellors had to say on a subject about which they knew nothing ; but, in spite of all the conjecturing of the sagest and oldest heads, the governor still continued to doubt.

Messengers were despatched to different places on the river ; but they returned without any tidings—the ship had made no port. Day after day, and week after week, elapsed ; but she never returned down the Hudson. As, however, the council seemed solicitous for intelligence, they had it in abundance. The captains of the sloops seldom arrived without bringing some report of having seen the strange ship at different parts of the river ; sometimes near the Palisadoes ;[2] sometimes off Croton Point, and sometimes in the highlands ; but she never was reported as having been seen above the highlands. The crews of the sloops, it is true, generally differed among themselves in their accounts of these apparitions ; but they may have arisen from the uncertain situations in which they saw her. Sometimes it was by the flashes of the thunder-storm

---

[1] Irving, in "Knickerbocker," laid great stress on Van Twiller's doubts. See p. 29.

[2] For these points on the Hudson see the map, p. 10.

lighting up a pitchy night, and giving glimpses of her career-ing across Tappaan Zee, or the wide waste of Haverstraw Bay. At one moment she would appear close upon them, as if likely to run them down, and would throw them into great bustle and alarm ; but the next flash would show her far off, always sailing against the wind. Sometimes, in quiet moonlight nights, she would be seen under some high bluff of the high-lands, all in deep shadow, excepting her top-sails glittering in the moonbeams ; by the time, however, that the voyagers would reach the place, there would be no ship to be seen ; and when they had passed on for some distance, and looked back, behold ! there she was again with her top-sails in the moon-shine ! Her appearance was always just after, or just before, or just in the midst of, unruly weather ; and she was known by all the skippers and voyagers of the Hudson, by the name of "the storm-ship."

These reports perplexed the governor and his council more than ever ; and it would be endless to repeat the conjectures and opinions that were uttered on the subject. Some quoted cases in point, of ships seen off the coast of New-England,[1] navigated by witches and goblins. Old Hans Van Pelt, who had been more than once to the Dutch Colony at the Cape of Good Hope, insisted that this must be the Flying Dutchman[2] which had so long haunted Table Bay,[3] but, being unable to make port, had now sought another harbor. Others sug-gested, that, if it really was a supernatural apparition, as there was every natural reason to believe, it might be Hen-drick Hudson, and his crew of the Half-Moon ; who, it was well-known, had once run aground in the upper part of the river, in seeking a north-west passage to China. This opinion had very little weight with the governor, but it passed current out of doors ; for indeed it had already been reported, that Hendrick Hudson and his crew haunted the Kaatskill Moun-

---

[1] Irving, in writing of the Dutch in New York, is very apt to mention New England witches.　　　[2] See p. 71.　　　[3] beneath Table Mountain.

tains,[1] and it appeared very reasonable to suppose, that his ship might infest the river, where the enterprise was baffled, or that it might bear the shadowy crew to their periodical revels in the mountain.

Other events occurred to occupy the thoughts and doubts of the sage Wouter and his council, and the storm-ship ceased to be a subject of deliberation at the board. It continued, however, to be a matter of popular belief and marvellous anecdote through the whole time of the Dutch government, and particularly just before the capture of New-Amsterdam,[2] and the subjugation of the province by the English squadron. About that time the storm-ship was repeatedly seen in the Tappaan Zee, and about Weehawk, and even down as far as Hoboken ; and her appearance was supposed to be ominous of the approaching squall in public affairs, and the downfall of Dutch domination.

Since that time, we have no authentic accounts of her ; though it is said she still haunts the highlands and cruises about Point-no-point. People who live along the river, insist that they sometimes see her in summer moonlight ; and that in a deep still midnight, they have heard the chant of her crew, as if heaving the lead ; but sighs and sounds are so deceptive along the mountainous shores, and about the wide bays and long reaches of this great river, that I confess I have very strong doubts upon the subject.

It is certain, nevertheless, that strange things have been seen in these highlands in storms, which are considered as connected with the old story of the ship. The captains of the river craft talk of a little bulbous-bottomed Dutch goblin, in trunk hose and sugar-loafed hat, with a speaking trumpet in his hand, which they say keeps about the Dunderberg.* They declare they have heard him, in stormy weather, in the midst

*

---

[1] Irving had already developed the legend of "Rip Van Winkle." The present spelling is Catskill.

[2] See p. 15.

* i.e., the "Thunder Mountain," so called from its echoes.

of the turmoil, giving orders in Low Dutch for the piping up of a fresh gust of wind, or the rattling off of another thunder-clap. That sometimes he has been seen surrounded by a crew of little imps in broad breeches and short doublets; tumbling head-over-heels in the rack and mist, and playing a thousand gambols in the air; or buzzing like a swarm of flies about Antony's Nose; and that, at such times, the hurry-scurry of the storm was always greatest. One time, a sloop, in passing by the Dunderberg, was overtaken by a thunder-gust, that came scouring round the mountain, and seemed to burst just over the vessel. Though tight and well ballasted, yet she labored dreadfully, until the water came over the gunwale. All the crew were amazed, when it was discovered that there was a little white sugar-loaf hat on the mast-head, which was known at once to be that of the Heer [1] of the Dunderberg. Nobody, however, dared to climb to the mast-head, and get rid of this terrible hat. The sloop continued laboring and rocking, as if she would have rolled her mast overboard. She seemed in continual danger either of upsetting or of running on shore. In this way she drove quite through the highlands, until she had passed Pollopol's Island, where, it is said, the jurisdiction of the Dunderberg potentate ceases. No sooner had she passed this bourne, than the little hat, all at once, spun up into the air like a top, whirled up all the clouds into a vortex, and hurried them back to the summit of Dunder-berg, while the sloop righted herself, and sailed on as quietly as if in a mill-pond. Nothing saved her from utter wreck, but the fortunate circumstance of having a horse-shoe nailed against the mast—a wise precaution against evil spirits, which has since been adopted by all the Dutch captains that navi-gate this haunted river.

There is another story told of this foul-weather urchin, by Skipper Daniel Ouslesticker, of Fish-Kill, who was never known to tell a lie. He declared, that, in a severe squall, he

[1] Dutch for "Mr." or "lord."

saw him seated astride of his bowsprit, riding the sloop ashore, full butt against Antony's Nose; and that he was exorcised by Dominie Van Gieson of Esopus,[1] who happened to be on board, and who sung the hymn of St. Nicholas; whereupon the goblin threw himself up in the air like a ball, and went off in a whirlwind, carrying away with him the nightcap of the dominie's wife ; which was discovered the next Sunday morning hanging on the weather-cock of Esopus church steeple, at least forty miles off ! After several events of this kind had taken place, the regular skippers of the river, for a long time, did not venture to pass the Dunderberg, without lowering their peaks,[2] out of homage to the Heer of the mountain ; and it was observed that all such as paid this tribute of respect were suffered to pass unmolested.[*]

[1] a town on the Hudson, now Kingston.

[2] The peak is the highest part of a fore-and-aft sail, and may be dropped without lowering the rest of the sail. It was a common sign of respect or token of inferiority at sea.

[*] Among the superstitions which prevailed in the colonies during the early times of the settlements, there seems to have been a singular one about phantom ships. The superstitious fancies of men are always apt to turn upon those objects which concern their daily occupations. The solitary ship, which, from year to year, came like a raven in the wilderness, bringing to the inhabitants of a settlement the comforts of life from the world from which they were cut off, was apt to be present to their dreams, whether sleeping or waking. The accidental sight from shore, of a sail gliding along the horizon, in those, as yet, lonely seas, was apt to be a matter of much talk and speculation. There is mention made in one of the early New-England writers, of a ship navigated by witches, with a great horse that stood by the mainmast. I have met with another story, somewhere, of a ship that drove on shore, in fair, sunny, tranquil weather, with sails all set, and a table spread in the cabin, as if to regale a number of guests, yet not a living being on board. These phantom ships always sailed in the eye of the wind ; or ploughed their way with great velocity, making the smooth sea foam before their bows, when not a breath of air was stirring.

Moore has finely wrought up one of these legends of the sea into a little tale which, within a small compass, contains the very essence of this species of supernatural fiction. I allude to his Spectre-Ship bound to Dead-man's Isle.—*Author's Note.*

V.—RIP VAN WINKLE.

A POSTHUMOUS[1] WRITING OF DIEDRICH KNICKERBOCKER.

> By Woden, God of Saxons,
> From whence comes Wensday, that is Wodensday,
> Truth is a thing that ever I will keep
> Unto thylke day in which I creep into
> My sepulchre—   CARTWRIGHT.

[The following Tale was found among the papers of the late Diedrich Knickerbocker,[2] an old gentleman of New-York, who was very curious in [3] the Dutch History of the province, and the manners of the descendants from its primitive settlers. His historical researches, however, did not lie so much among books as among men; for the former are lamentably scanty on his favorite topics; whereas he found the old burghers, and still more, their wives, rich in that legendary lore, so invaluable to true history. Whenever, therefore, he happened upon a genuine Dutch family, snugly shut up in its low-roofed farm-house,[4] under a spreading sycamore, he looked upon it as a little clasped volume of black-letter, and studied it with the zeal of a bookworm.

The result of all these researches was a history of the province, during the reign of the Dutch governors, which he published some years since. There have been various opinions as to the literary character of his work, and, to tell the truth, it is not a whit better than it should be. Its chief merit is its scrupulous accuracy, which, indeed, was a little questioned, on its first appearance, but has since been completely established; and it is now admitted into all historical collections, as a book of unquestionable authority.[5]

[1] published after the author's death.
[2] See p. 17.
[3] Is not this an unusual construction?
[4] See " Wolfert's Roost," p. 75.
[5] We must remember, on reading this paragraph, that Irving was himself the author of the book, and that as literature it is highly esteemed and as history not at all. See the Introduction, p. 16.

The old gentleman died shortly after the publication of his work, and now, that he is dead and gone, it cannot do much harm to his memory, to say, that his time might have been much better employed in weightier labors. He, however, was apt to ride his hobby his own way; and though it did now and then kick up the dust a little in the eyes of his neighbors, and grieve the spirit of some friends for whom he felt the truest deference and affection, yet his errors and follies are remembered "more in sorrow than in anger," and it begins to be suspected, that he never intended to injure or offend. But however his memory may be appreciated by critics, it is still held dear among many folk, whose good opinion is well worth having; particularly by certain biscuit-bakers, who have gone so far as to imprint his likeness on their new-year cakes, and have thus given him a chance for immortality, almost equal to the being stamped on a Waterloo medal, or a Queen Anne's farthing.]

WHOEVER has made a voyage up the Hudson, must remember the Kaatskill[1] Mountains. They are a dismembered branch of the great Appalachian family, and are seen away to the west of the river, swelling up to a noble height, and lording it over the surrounding country. Every change of season, every change of weather, indeed every hour of the day produces some change in the magical hues and shapes of these mountains; and they are regarded by all the good wives, far and near, as perfect barometers. When the weather is fair and settled, they are clothed in blue and purple, and print their bold outlines on the clear evening sky; but sometimes, when the rest of the landscape is cloudless, they will gather a hood of gray vapors about their summits, which in the last rays of the setting sun, will glow and light up like a crown of glory.

At the foot of these fairy mountains, the voyager may have

_____
[1] now more commonly spelled Catskill.

descried the light smoke curling up from a village,[1] whose
shingle roofs gleam among the trees, just where the blue tints
of the upland melt away into the fresh green of the nearer
landscape. It is a little village of great antiquity, having
been founded by some of the Dutch colonists, in the early
times of the province, just about the beginning of the government of the good Peter Stuyvesant (may he rest in peace !),
and there were some of the houses of the original settlers
standing within a few years, built of small yellow bricks,
brought from Holland, having latticed windows and gable
fronts, surmounted with weathercocks.

In that same village, and in one of these very houses
(which, to tell the precise truth, was sadly time-worn and
weather-beaten), there lived many years since, while the
country was yet a province of Great Britain, a simple, good-
natured fellow, of the name of Rip Van Winkle. He was a
descendant of the Van Winkles who figured so gallantly in
the chivalrous days of Peter Stuyvesant, and accompanied
him to the siege of fort Christina.[2] He inherited, however,
but little of the martial character of his ancestors. I have
observed that he was a simple, good-natured man ; he was
moreover a kind neighbor, and an obedient henpecked husband. Indeed, to the latter circumstance might be owing
that meekness of spirit which gained him such universal pop-
ularity ; for those men are most apt to be obsequious and
conciliating abroad, who are under the discipline of shrews
at home. Their tempers, doubtless, are rendered pliant and
malleable in the fiery furnace of domestic tribulation, and a
curtain lecture is worth all the sermons in the world for
teaching the virtues of patience and long-suffering. A termagant[3] wife may, therefore, in some respects, be considered

---

[1] Irving had no special village in mind,
for at this time (1819) he had seen the Catskills only from the river. In 1832, on his
return from Europe, he visited the Catskills
for the first time. See p. 19.

[2] a Swedish settlement on the Delaware.
See p. 14.

[3] As a noun, the word means a brawling
woman ; but it is often used as an ad-
jective.

a tolerable blessing; and if so, Rip Van Winkle was thrice blessed.

Certain it is, that he was a great favorite among all the good wives of the village, who, as usual with the amiable sex, took his part in all family squabbles, and never failed, whenever they talked those matters over in their evening gossipings, to lay all the blame on Dame Van Winkle. The children of the village, too, would shout with joy whenever he approached. He assisted at their sports, made their playthings, taught them to fly kites and shoot marbles, and told them long stories of ghosts, witches, and Indians. Whenever he went dodging about the village, he was surrounded by a troop of them hanging on his skirts, clambering on his back, and playing a thousand tricks on him with impunity; and not a dog would bark at him throughout the neighborhood.

The great error in Rip's composition was an insuperable aversion to all kinds of profitable labor. It could not be from the want of assiduity or perseverance; for he would sit on a wet rock, with a rod as long and heavy as a Tartar's lance, and fish all day without a murmur, even though he should not be encouraged by a single nibble. He would carry a fowling-piece on his shoulder, for hours together, trudging through woods and swamps, and up hill and down dale, to shoot a few squirrels or wild pigeons. He would never refuse to assist a neighbor even in the roughest toil, and was a foremost man at all country frolics for husking Indian corn, or building stone fences. The women of the village, too, used to employ him to run their errands, and to do such little odd jobs as their less obliging husbands would not do for them;— in a word, Rip was ready to attend to anybody's business but his own; but as to doing family duty, and keeping his farm in order, he found it impossible.

In fact, he declared it was of no use to work on his farm; it was the most pestilent little piece of ground in the whole country; everything about it went wrong, and would go wrong in spite of him. His fences were continually falling to pieces; his cow would either go astray, or get among the cabbages; weeds were sure to grow quicker in his fields that anywhere else; the rain always made a point of setting in just as he had some out-door work to do; so that though his patrimonial estate had dwindled away under his management, acre by acre, until there was little more left than a mere patch of Indian corn and potatoes, yet it was the worst conditioned farm in the neighborhood.

His children, too, were as ragged and wild as if they belonged to nobody. His son Rip, an urchin begotten in his own likeness, promised to inherit the habits, with the old clothes of his father. He was generally seen trooping like a colt at his mother's heels, equipped in a pair of his father's cast-off galligaskins,¹ which he had much ado to hold up with one hand, as a fine lady does her train in bad weather.

Rip Van Winkle, however, was one of those happy mortals, of foolish, well-oiled dispositions, who take the world easy, eat white bread or brown, whichever can be got with least thought or trouble, and would rather starve on a penny than work for a pound. If left to himself, he would have whistled life away, in perfect contentment; but his wife kept continually dinning in his ears about his idleness, his carelessness, and the ruin he was bringing on his family.

Morning, noon, and night, her tongue was incessantly going, and everything he said or did was sure to produce a torrent of household eloquence. Rip had but one way of replying to all lectures of the kind, and that, by frequent use, had grown into a habit. He shrugged his shoulders, shook his head, cast up his eyes, but said nothing. This, however, always provoked a fresh volley from his wife, so that he was fain to draw off his forces, and take to the outside of the house—the only side which, in truth, belongs to a henpecked husband.²

¹ breeches.
² Irving presents Mrs. Van Winkle as a shrew, but there can be no doubt that she had the right on her side.

Rip's sole domestic adherent was his dog Wolf, who was as much henpecked as his master; for Dame Van Winkle regarded them as companions in idleness, and even looked upon Wolf with an evil eye, as the cause of his master's going so often astray. True it is, in all points of spirit befitting an honorable dog, he was as courageous an animal as ever scoured the woods—but what courage can withstand the ever-during and all-besetting terrors of a woman's tongue? The moment Wolf entered the house, his crest fell, his tail drooped to the ground, or curled between his legs, he sneaked about with a gallows air, casting many a sidelong glance at Dame Van Winkle, and at the least flourish of a broomstick or ladle, he would fly to the door with yelping precipitation.

Time grew worse and worse with Rip Van Winkle, as years of matrimony rolled on: a tart temper never mellows with age, and a sharp tongue is the only edge tool that grows keener with constant use. For a long while he used to console himself, when driven from home, by frequenting a kind of perpetual club of the sages, philosophers, and other idle personages of the village, which held its sessions on a bench before a small inn, designated by a rubicund portrait of his majesty George the Third. Here they used to sit in the shade of a long lazy summer's day, talking listlessly over village gossip, or telling endless sleepy stories about nothing. But it would have been worth any statesman's money to have heard the profound discussions which sometimes took place, when by chance an old newspaper fell into their hands, from some passing traveller. How solemnly they would listen to the contents, as drawled out by Derrick Van Bummel, the schoolmaster, a dapper, learned little man, who was not to be daunted by the most gigantic word in the dictionary; and how sagely they would deliberate upon public events some months after they had taken place.

The opinions of this junto' were completely controlled by

' a private gathering; especially, as the word is used in English, for political purposes.

Nicholas Vedder, a patriarch of the village, and landlord of the inn, at the door of which he took his seat from morning till night, just moving sufficiently to avoid the sun, and keep in the shade of a large tree; so that the neighbors could tell the hour by his movements as accurately as by a sun-dial.[1] It is true, he was rarely heard to speak, but smoked his pipe incessantly. His adherents, however, (for every great man has his adherents,) perfectly understood him, and knew how to gather his opinions. When anything that was read or related displeased him, he was observed to smoke his pipe vehemently, and to send forth short, frequent, and angry puffs; but when pleased, he would inhale the smoke slowly and tranquilly, and emit it in light and placid clouds, and sometimes taking the pipe from his mouth, and letting the fragrant vapor curl about his nose, would gravely nod his head in token of perfect approbation.

From even this stronghold the unlucky Rip was at length routed by his termagant wife, who would suddenly break in upon the tranquillity of the assemblage, and call the members all to nought; nor was that august personage, Nicholas Vedder himself, sacred from the daring tongue of this terrible virago,[2] who charged him outright with encouraging her husband in habits of idleness.

Poor Rip was at last reduced almost to despair, and his only alternative to escape from the labor of the farm and the clamor of his wife, was to take gun in hand, and stroll away into the woods. Here he would sometimes seat himself at the foot of a tree, and share the contents of his wallet with Wolf, with whom he sympathized as a fellow-sufferer in persecution. "Poor Wolf," he would say, "thy mistress leads thee a dog's life of it; but never mind, my lad, whilst I live thou shalt never want a friend to stand by thee!" Wolf would wag his tail, look wistfully in his master's face, and if dogs can feel

---

[1] In olden times, when watches and clocks were less common, sun-dials were very usual means of telling time.　　　　[2] a fierce and masculine woman.

pity, I verily believe he reciprocated the sentiment with all his heart.

In a long ramble of the kind, on a fine autumnal day, Rip had unconsciously scrambled to one of the highest parts of the Kaatskill Mountains. He was after his favorite sport of squirrel-shooting, and the still solitudes had echoed and re-echoed with the reports of his gun. Panting and fatigued, he threw himself, late in the afternoon, on a green knoll[1] covered with mountain herbage, that crowned the brow of a precipice. From an opening between the trees, he could overlook all the lower country for many a mile of rich woodland. He saw at a distance the lordly Hudson, far, far below him, moving on its silent but majestic course, with the reflection of a purple cloud, or the sail of a lagging bark, here and there sleeping on its glassy bosom, and at last losing itself in the blue highlands.

On the other side he looked down into a deep mountain glen, wild, lonely, and shagged, the bottom filled with frag-ments from the impending cliffs, and scarcely lighted by the reflected rays of the setting sun. For some time Rip lay mus-ing on this scene; evening was gradually advancing; the mountains began to throw their long blue shadows over the valleys; he saw that it would be dark long before he could reach the village; and he heaved a heavy sigh when he thought of encountering the terrors of Dame Van Winkle.

As he was about to descend he heard a voice from a dis-tance hallooing, " Rip Van Winkle ! Rip Van Winkle !" He looked around, but could see nothing but a crow winging its solitary flight across the mountain. He thought his fancy must have deceived him, and turned again to descend, when he heard the same cry ring through the still evening air, " Rip

---

[1] The local tradition points out a spot about half-way up on the eastern slope of Catskill Mountain. Irving, however, had no especial place in mind; at this time he had never explored the Catskills himself. His description, therefore, cannot be easily veri-fied. In 1832, years after the story was written, he visited Catskill Mountain for the first time and saw " the waterfall, glen, etc., that are pointed out as the veritable haunts of Rip Van Winkle." He found the wild scenery of the mountains to be far beyond his conception.

Van Winkle! Rip Van Winkle!"—at the same time Wolf bristled up his back, and giving a low growl, skulked to his master's side, looking fearfully down into the glen. Rip now felt a vague apprehension stealing over him ; he looked anxiously in the same direction, and perceived a strange figure slowly toiling up the rocks, and bending under the weight of something he carried on his back. He was surprised to see any human being in this lonely and unfrequented place, but supposing it to be some one of the neighborhood in need of his assistance, he hastened down to yield it.

On nearer approach, he was still more surprised at the singularity of the stranger's appearance. He was a short square-built old fellow, with thick bushy hair, and a grizzled beard. His dress was of the antique Dutch fashion—a cloth jerkin strapped round the waist—several pair of breeches,[1] the outer one of ample volume, decorated with rows of buttons down the sides, and bunches at the knees. He bore on his shoulders a stout keg, that seemed full of liquor, and made signs for Rip to approach and assist him with the load. Though rather shy and distrustful of this new acquaintance, Rip complied with his usual alacrity, and mutually relieving each other, they clambered up a narrow gully, apparently the dry bed of a mountain torrent. As they ascended, Rip every now and then heard long rolling peals, like distant thunder, that seemed to issue out of a deep ravine, or rather cleft between lofty rocks, toward which their rugged path conducted. He paused for an instant, but supposing it to be the muttering of one of those transient thunder-showers which often take place in the mountain heights, he proceeded. Passing through the ravine, they came to a hollow, like a small amphitheatre, surrounded by perpendicular precipices, over the brinks of which, impending trees shot their branches, so that you only caught glimpses of the azure sky, and the bright evening cloud.

---

[1] Irving delighted to call attention to what he insisted was the Dutch habit of wearing many pairs of breeches or many petticoats. See p. 42.

During the whole time, Rip and his companion had labored on in silence; for though the former marvelled greatly what could be the object of carrying a keg of liquor up this wild mountain, yet there was something strange and incomprehensible about the unknown, that inspired awe, and checked familiarity.

On entering the amphitheatre, new objects of wonder presented themselves. On a level spot in the centre was a company of odd-looking personages playing at nine-pins. They were dressed in a quaint outlandish fashion : some wore short doublets, others jerkins, with long knives in their belts, and most of them had enormous breeches, of similar style with that of the guide's. Their visages too, were peculiar : one had a large head, broad face, and small piggish eyes ; the face of another seemed to consist entirely of nose, and was surmounted by a white sugar-loaf [1] hat, set off with a little red cock's tail. They all had beards, of various shapes and colors. There was one who seemed to be the commander. He was a stout old gentleman, with a weather-beaten countenance ; he wore a laced doublet, broad belt and hanger, high-crowned hat and feather, red stockings, and high-heeled shoes, with roses in them. The whole group reminded Rip of the figures in an old Flemish painting, in the parlor of Dominie Van Schaick, the village parson, and which had been brought over from Holland at the time of the settlement.

What seemed particularly odd to Rip was, that though these folks were evidently amusing themselves, yet they maintained the gravest faces, the most mysterious silence, and were, withal, the most melancholy party of pleasure he had ever witnessed. Nothing interrupted the stillness of the scene but the noise of the balls, which, whenever they were rolled, echoed along the mountains like rumbling peals of thunder.

As Rip and his companion approached them, they sud-

---

[1] Sugar-loaves are uncommon nowadays. A sugar-loaf hat had a high, pointed crown. Cf. p. 83.

denly desisted from their play, and stared at him with such a fixed statue-like gaze, and such strange, uncouth, lack-lustre countenances, that his heart turned within him, and his knees smote together. His companion now emptied the contents of the keg into large flagons, and made signs to him to wait upon the company. He obeyed with fear and trembling; they quaffed the liquor in profound silence, and then returned to their game.

By degrees, Rip's awe and apprehension subsided. He even ventured, when no eye was fixed upon him, to taste the beverage, which he found had much of the flavor of excellent Hollands. He was naturally a thirsty soul, and was soon tempted to repeat the draught. One taste provoked another, and he reiterated his visits to the flagon so often, that at length his senses were overpowered, his eyes swam in his head, his head gradually declined, and he fell into a deep sleep.

On waking, he found himself on the green knoll from whence he had first seen the old man of the glen. He rubbed his eyes—it was a bright sunny morning. The birds were hopping and twittering among the bushes, and the eagle was wheeling aloft, and breasting the pure mountain breeze. " Surely," thought Rip, " I have not slept here all night." He recalled the occurrences before he fell asleep. The strange man with the keg of liquor—the mountain ravine—the wild retreat among the rocks—the wo-begone party at nine-pins— the flagon—" Oh ! that wicked flagon !" thought Rip—" what excuse shall I make to Dame Van Winkle ?"

He looked round for his gun, but in place of the clean well-oiled fowling-piece, he found an old firelock [1] lying by him, the barrel encrusted with rust, the lock falling off, and the stock worm-eaten. He now suspected that the grave roysterers of the mountain had put a trick up on him, and having dosed him with liquor, had robbed him of his gun. Wolf, too, had disappeared, but he might have strayed away after a squir-

[1] more commonly called a flintlock.

rel or partridge. He whistled after him and shouted his name, but all in vain; the echoes repeated his whistle and shout, but no dog was to be seen.

He determined to revisit the scene of the last evening's gambol, and if he met with any of the party, to demand his dog and gun. As he rose to walk, he found himself stiff in the joints, and wanting in his usual activity. "These mountain beds do not agree with me," thought Rip, "and if this frolic should lay me up with a fit of the rheumatism, I shall have a blessed time with Dame Van Winkle." With some difficulty he got down into the glen; he found the gully up which he and his companion had ascended the preceding evening; but to his astonishment a mountain stream was now foaming down it, leaping from rock to rock, and filling the glen with babbling murmurs. He, however, made shift to scramble up its sides, working his toilsome way through thickets of birch, sassafras, and witch-hazel; and sometimes tripped up or entangled by the wild grape vines that twisted their coils and tendrils from tree to tree, and spread a kind of network in his path.

At length he reached to where the ravine had opened through the cliffs to the amphitheatre; but no traces of such opening remained. The rocks presented a high impenetrable wall, over which the torrent came tumbling in a sheet of feathery foam, and fell into a broad deep basin, black from the shadows of the surrounding forest. Here, then, poor Rip was brought to a stand. He again called and whistled after his dog; he was only answered by the cawing of a flock of idle crows, sporting high in the air about a dry tree that overhung a sunny precipice; and who, secure in their elevation, seemed to look down and scoff at the poor man's perplexities. What was to be done? The morning was passing away, and Rip felt famished for want of his breakfast. He grieved to give up his dog and gun; he dreaded to meet his wife; but it would not do to starve among the mountains.

He shook his head, shouldered the rusty firelock, and, with a heart full of trouble and anxiety, turned his steps homeward.

As he approached the village, he met a number of people, but none whom he knew, which somewhat surprised him, for he had thought himself acquainted with every one in the country round. Their dress, too, was of a different fashion from that to which he was accustomed. They all stared at him with equal marks of surprise, and whenever they cast eyes upon him, invariably stroked their chins. The constant recurrence of this gesture, induced Rip, involuntarily, to do the same, when, to his astonishment, he found his beard had grown a foot long!

He had now entered the skirts of the village. A troop of strange children ran at his heels, hooting after him, and pointing at his gray beard. The dogs, too, not one of which he recognized for an old acquaintance, barked at him as he passed. The very village was altered : it was larger and more populous. There were rows of houses which he had never seen before, and those which had been his familiar haunts had disappeared. Strange names were over the doors—strange faces at the windows—everything was strange. His mind now misgave him ; he began to doubt whether both he and the world around him were not bewitched. Surely this was his native village, which he had left but a day before. There stood the Kaatskill Mountains—there ran the silver Hudson at a distance—there was every hill and dale precisely as it had always been—Rip was sorely perplexed—"That flagon last night," thought he, " has addled my poor head sadly !"

It was with some difficulty that he found the way to his own house, which he approached with silent awe, expecting every moment to hear the shrill voice of Dame Van Winkle. He found the house gone to decay—the roof fallen in, the windows shattered, and the doors off the hinges. A half-starved dog, that looked like Wolf, was skulking about it. Rip called him by name, but the cur snarled, showed his

7

teeth, and passed on. This was an unkind cut indeed.—" My very dog," sighed poor Rip, " has forgotten me ! "

He entered the house, which, to tell the truth, Dame Van Winkle had always kept in neat order. It was empty, forlorn, and apparently abandoned. This desolateness overcame all his connubial fears—he called loudly for his wife and children —the lonely chambers rang for a moment with his voice, and then all again was silence.

He now hurried forth, and hastened to his old resort, the village inn—but it too was gone. A large rickety wooden building stood in its place, with great gaping windows, some of them broken, and mended with old hats and petticoats, and over the door was painted, " The Union Hotel, by Jonathan Doolittle." Instead of the great tree that used to shelter the quiet little Dutch inn of yore, there now was reared a tall naked pole, with something on the top that looked like a red night-cap,[1] and from it was fluttering a flag, on which was a singular assemblage of stars and stripes [2]—all this was strange and incomprehensible. He recognized on the sign, however, the ruby face of King George, under which he had smoked so many a peaceful pipe, but even this was singularly metamorphosed. The red coat was changed for one of blue and buff, a sword was held in the hand instead of a sceptre, the head was decorated with a cocked hat, and underneath was painted in large characters, GENERAL WASHINGTON.

There was, as usual, a crowd of folk about the door, but none that Rip recollected. The very character of the people seemed changed. There was a busy, bustling, disputatious tone about it, instead of the accustomed phlegm and drowsy tranquillity. He looked in vain for the sage Nicholas Vedder,· with his broad face, double chin, and fair long pipe, uttering clouds of tobacco smoke, instead of idle speeches; or Van Bummel, the schoolmaster, doling forth the contents of an

[1] It was a Liberty cap.
[2] It was singular only to Rip Van Winkle, of course, who had never before seen the · Stars and Stripes.

ancient newspaper. In place of these, a lean bilious-looking
fellow, with his pockets full of handbills, was haranguing
vehemently about rights of citizens—election—members of
Congress—liberty—Bunker's hill—heroes of seventy-six—
and other words, that were a perfect Babylonish jargon to the
bewildered Van Winkle.

The appearance of Rip, with his long, grizzled beard, his
rusty fowling-piece, his uncouth dress, and the army of women
and children that had gathered at his heels, soon attracted the
attention of the tavern politicians. They crowded round him,
eyeing him from head to foot, with great curiosity. The
orator bustled up to him, and drawing him partly aside, inquired, "On which side he voted?" Rip stared in vacant
stupidity. Another short but busy little fellow pulled him by
the arm, and rising on tiptoe, inquired in his ear, "Whether
he was Federal or Democrat."[1] Rip was equally at a loss to
comprehend the question; when a knowing, self-important old
gentleman, in a sharp cocked hat, made his way through the
crowd, putting them to the right and left with his elbows as
he passed, and planting himself before Van Winkle, with one
arm a-kimbo, the other resting on his cane, his keen eyes
and sharp hat penetrating, as it were, into his very soul, demanded in an austere tone, "What brought him to the election with a gun on his shoulder, and a mob at his heels, and
whether he meant to breed a riot in the village?"

"Alas! gentlemen," cried Rip, somewhat dismayed, "I am
a poor, quiet man, a native of the place, and a loyal subject
of the King, God bless him!"

Here a general shout burst from the bystanders—"a tory![2]
a tory! a spy! a refugee! hustle him! away with him!"

It was with great difficulty that the self-important man in
the cocked hat restored order; and having assumed a tenfold

---

[1] the early party-names in the United
States. The Federalists believed in a strong
general government; the Democrats believed that political power should remain as
near the people as possible. The Federalist
party, as such, has now passed away.

[2] The adherents of the English in the
Revolution were called Tories.

austerity of brow, demanded again of the unknown culprit, what he came there for, and whom he was seeking. The poor man humbly assured him that he meant no harm, but merely came there in search of some of his neighbors, who used to keep about the tavern.

"Well—who are they ?—name them."

Rip bethought himself a moment, and inquired, "Where's Nicholas Vedder ?"

There was a silence for a little while, when an old man replied, in a thin, piping voice, "Nicholas Vedder ? why, he is dead and gone these eighteen years ! There was a wooden tomb-stone in the church-yard that used to tell all about him, but that's rotten and gone too."

"Where's Brom Dutcher ?"

"Oh, he went off to the army in the beginning of the war ; some say he was killed at the storming of Stony-Point [1]—others say he was drowned in the squall, at the foot of Antony's Nose. I don't know—he never came back again."

"Where's Van Bummel, the schoolmaster ?"

"He went off to the wars, too ; was a great militia general, and is now in Congress."

Rip's heart died away, at hearing of these sad changes in his home and friends, and finding himself thus alone in the world. Every answer puzzled him, too, by treating of such enormous lapses of time, and of matters which he could not understand : war—Congress—Stony-Point !—he had no courage to ask after any more friends, but cried out in despair, "Does nobody here know Rip Van Winkle ?"

"Oh, Rip Van Winkle !" exclaimed two or three. "Oh, to be sure ! that's Rip Van Winkle yonder, leaning against the tree."

Rip looked, and beheld a precise counterpart of himself as he went up the mountain ; apparently as lazy, and certainly

[1] The British position on Stony Point was taken by storm, July 15, 1779, by General Anthony Wayne. For these places, consult the map, p. 10.

as ragged. The poor fellow was now completely confounded. He doubted his own identity, and whether he was himself or another man. In the midst of his bewilderment, the man in the cocked hat demanded who he was, and what was his name?

"God knows," exclaimed he at his wit's end; "I'm not myself—I'm somebody else—that's me yonder—no—that's somebody else, got into my shoes—I was myself last night, but I fell asleep on the mountain, and they've changed my gun, and everything's changed, and I'm changed, and I can't tell what's my name, or who I am!"

The bystanders began now to look at each other, nod, wink significantly, and tap their fingers against their foreheads.[1] There was a whisper, also, about securing the gun, and keeping the old fellow from doing mischief; at the very suggestion of which, the self-important man with the cocked hat retired with some precipitation. At this critical moment a fresh comely woman passed through the throng to get a peep at the gray-bearded man. She had a chubby child in her arms, which, frightened at his looks, began to cry, "Hush, Rip," cried she, "hush, you little fool; the old man won't hurt you." The name of the child, the air of the mother, the tone of her voice, all awakened a train of recollections in his mind.

"What is your name, my good woman?" asked he.

"Judith Gardenier."

"And your father's name?"

"Ah, poor man, his name was Rip Van Winkle; its twenty years since he went away from home with his gun, and never has been heard of since—his dog came home without him; but whether he shot himself, or was carried away by the Indians, nobody can tell. I was then but a little girl."

Rip had but one question more to ask; but he put it with a faltering voice:

---

[1] They meant that he was weak in the head.

"Where's your mother?"

Oh, she too had died but a short time since : she broke a blood-vessel in a fit of passion at a New-England pedler.

There was a drop of comfort, at least, in this intelligence. The honest man could contain himself no longer. He caught his daughter and her child in his arms. "I am your father!" cried he—"Young Rip Van Winkle once—old Rip Van Winkle now—Does nobody know poor Rip Van Winkle!"

All stood amazed, until an old woman, tottering out from among the crowd, put her hand to her brow, and peering under it in his face for a moment, exclaimed, "Sure enough! it is Rip Van Winkle—it is himself. Welcome home again, old neighbor—Why, where have you been these twenty long years?"

Rip's story was soon told, for the whole twenty years had been to him but as one night. The neighbors stared when they heard it; some were seen to wink at each other, and put their tongues in their cheeks; and the self-important man in the cocked hat, who, when the alarm was over, had returned to the field, screwed down the corners of his mouth, and shook his head—upon which there was a general shaking of the head throughout the assemblage.

It was determined, however, to take the opinion of old Peter Vanderdonk, who was seen slowly advancing up the road. He was a descendant of the historian of that name,[1] who wrote one of the earliest accounts of the province. Peter was the most ancient inhabitant of the village, and well versed in all the wonderful events and traditions of the neighborhood. He recollected Rip at once, and corroborated his story in the most satisfactory manner. He assured the company that it was a fact, handed down from his ancestor the historian, that the Kaatskill Mountains had always been haunted by strange beings. That it was affirmed that the great Hendrick Hudson, the first discoverer of the river and country, kept a kind .

---

[1] Adrian van der Donck published his "Description of New Netherland" in 1656.

of vigil there every twenty years, with his crew of the Half-moon, being permitted in this way to revisit the scenes of his enterprise, and keep a guardian eye upon the river and the great city called by his name.¹ That his father had once seen them in their old Dutch dresses playing at nine-pins in the hollow of the mountain ; and that he himself had heard, one summer afternoon, the sound of their balls, like distant peals of thunder.

To make a long story short, the company broke up, and returned to the more important concerns of the election. Rip's daughter took him home to live with her ; she had a snug, well-furnished house, and a stout cheery farmer for a husband, whom Rip recollected for one of the urchins that used to climb upon his back. As to Rip's son and heir, who was the ditto of himself, seen leaning against the tree, he was employed to work on the farm ; but evinced a hereditary dis-position to attend to anything else but his business.

Rip now resumed his old walks and habits ; he soon found many of his former cronies, though all rather the worse for the wear and tear of time ; and preferred making friends among the rising generation, with whom he soon grew into great favor.

Having nothing to do at home, and being arrived at that happy age when a man can do nothing with impunity, he took his place once more on the bench, at the inn door, and was reverenced as one of the patriarchs of the village, and a chronicle of the old times "before the war." It was some time before he could get into the regular track of gossip, or could be made to comprehend the strange events that had taken place during his torpor. How that there had been a revolutionary war—that the country had thrown off the yoke of old England—and that, instead of being a subject of his majesty George the Third, he was now a free citizen of the

¹ Irving must have been thinking chiefly of the river. The city of Hudson is on the other side of the river and farther up.

United States. Rip, in fact, was no politician; the changes of states and empires made but little impression on him; but there was one species of despotism under which he had long groaned, and that was — petticoat government. Happily, that was at an end; he had got his neck out of the yoke of matrimony, and could go in and out whenever he pleased, without dreading the tyranny of Dame Van Winkle. Whenever her name was mentioned, however, he shook his head, shrugged his shoulders, and cast up his eyes; which might pass either for an expression of resignation to his fate, or joy at his deliverance.

He used to tell his story to every stranger that arrived at Mr. Doolittle's hotel. He was observed, at first, to vary on some points every time he told it, which was doubtless owing to his having so recently awaked. It at last settled down precisely to the tale I have related, and not a man, woman, or child in the neighborhood, but knew it by heart. Some always pretended to doubt the reality of it, and insisted that Rip had been out of his head, and that this was one point on which he always remained flighty. The old Dutch inhabitants, however, almost universally gave it full credit. Even to this day, they never hear a thunder-storm of a summer afternoon about the Kaatskill, but they say Hendrick Hudson and his crew are at their game of nine-pins; and it is a common wish of all henpecked husbands in the neighborhood when life hangs heavy on their hands, that they might have a quieting draught out of Rip Van Winkle's flagon.

NOTE BY INVING.—The foregoing tale, one would suspect, had been suggested to Mr. Knickerbocker by a little German superstition about the Emperor Frederick *der Rothbart* and the Kyffhäuser mountain;[1] the subjoined note, however, which he had appended to the tale, shows that it is an absolute fact, narrated with his usual fidelity.

"The story of Rip Van Winkle may seem incredible to many, but nevertheless I give it my full belief, for I know the vicinity of our old Dutch settlements to have been very subject to marvellous events and appearances. Indeed, I have heard many stranger stories than this, in the villages along the Hudson; all of which were too well authenticated to admit of a doubt. I have even talked with Rip Van Winkle myself, who, when last I saw him, was a very venerable old man, and so perfectly ra-

[1] See "Wolfert's Roost," p. 60, note.

VI.—THE LEGEND OF SLEEPY HOLLOW.

(FOUND AMONG THE PAPERS OF THE LATE DIEDRICH KNICKERBOCKER.)

A pleasing land of drowsy head it was,
Of dreams that wave before the half-shut eye ;
And of gay castles in the clouds that pass,
Forever flushing round a summer sky.
—*Castle of Indolence.*

In the bosom of one of those spacious coves which indent the eastern shore of the Hudson, at that broad expansion of the river denominated by the ancient Dutch navigators the Tappaan Zee,[1] and where they always prudently shortened sail, and implored the protection of St. Nicholas when they crossed, there lies a small market town or rural port, which by some is called Greenburgh, but which is more generally and properly known by the name of Tarry Town. This name was given it, we are told, in former days, by the good housewives of the adjacent country, from the inveterate propensity of their husbands to linger about the village tavern on market days. Be that as it may, I do not vouch for the fact, but merely advert to it, for the sake of being precise and authentic. Not far from this village, perhaps about three miles, there is a little valley or rather lap of land among high hills, which is one of the quietest places in the whole world. A small brook glides through it, with just murmur enough to lull one to repose ; and the occasional whistle of a quail, or tapping of a woodpecker, is almost the only sound that ever breaks in upon the uniform tranquillity.

tional and consistent on every other point, that I think no conscientious person could refuse to take this into the bargain ; nay, I have seen a certificate on the subject taken before a country justice, and signed with a cross, in the justice's own handwriting.

The story, therefore, is beyond the possibility of doubt."

[1] The name "Tappaan" appears on very early maps ; *e.g.*, De Leat's of 1630, and Van der Donck's of 1656.

I recollect that, when a stripling, my first exploit in squirrel-shooting[1] was in a grove of tall walnut-trees that shades one side of the valley. I had wandered into it at noon-time, when all nature is peculiarly quiet, and was startled by the roar of my own gun, as it broke the sabbath stillness around, and was prolonged and reverberated by the angry echoes. If ever I should wish for a retreat whither I might steal from the world and its distractions, and dream quietly away the remnant of a troubled life, I know of none more promising than this little valley.

From the listless repose of the place, and the peculiar character of its inhabitants, who are descendants from the original Dutch settlers, this sequestered glen has long been known by the name of SLEEPY HOLLOW, and its rustic lads are called the Sleepy Hollow Boys throughout all the neighboring country. A drowsy, dreamy influence seems to hang over the land, and to pervade the very atmosphere. Some say that the place was bewitched by a high German[2] doctor, during the early days of the settlement; others, that an old Indian chief, the prophet or wizard of his tribe, held his pow-wows[3] there before the country was discovered by Master Hendrick Hudson. Certain it is the place still continues under the sway of some witching power, that holds a spell over the minds of the good people, causing them to walk in a continual reverie. They are given to all kinds of marvellous beliefs; are subject to trances and visions, and frequently see strange sights, and hear music and voices in the air. The whole neighborhood abounds with local tales, haunted spots, and twilight superstitions; stars shoot and meteors glare oftener across the valley than in any other part of the country, and the night-mare, with her whole nine fold, seems to make it the favorite scene of her gambols.

[1] See p. 19.

[2] The Dutch are Low German (down near the sea). Up toward the mountains the people may be called High German.

[3] Originally the word meant an Indian wizard. It was transferred to his incantations and consultations, and now has chiefly the latter sense.

The dominant spirit, however, that haunts this enchanted region, and seems to be commander-in-chief of all the powers of the air, is the apparition of a figure on horseback without a head. It is said by some to be the ghost of a Hessian [1] trooper, whose head had been carried away by a cannon-ball, in some nameless battle during the revolutionary war, and who is ever and anon seen by the country folk, hurrying along in the gloom of night, as if on the wings of the wind. His haunts are not confined to the valley, but extend at times to the adjacent roads, and especially to the vicinity of a church that is at no great distance. Indeed, certain of the most authentic historians of those parts, who have been careful in collecting and collating the floating facts concerning this spectre, allege, that the body of the trooper having been in the churchyard, the ghost rides forth to the scene of battle in nightly quest of his head, and that the rushing speed with which he sometimes passes along the hollow, like a midnight blast, is owing to his being belated, and in a hurry to get back to the churchyard before daybreak.

Such is the general purport of this legendary superstition, which has furnished materials for many a wild story in that region of shadows; and the spectre is known at all the country firesides, by the name of The Headless Horseman of Sleepy Hollow.

It is remarkable, that the visionary propensity I have mentioned is not confined to the native inhabitants of the valley, but is unconsciously imbibed by everyone who resides there for a time. However wide awake they may have been before they entered that sleepy region, they are sure, in a little time, to inhale the witching influence of the air, and begin to grow imaginative—to dream dreams, and see apparitions.

I mention this peaceful spot with all possible laud [2]; for it is in such little retired Dutch valleys, found here and there

---

[1] The Hessians were soldiers hired by England from the Elector of Hesse-Cassel.
[2] praise.

embosomed in the great State of New-York, that population, manners, and customs remain fixed, while the great torrent of migration and improvement, which is making such incessant changes in other parts of this restless country, sweeps by them unobserved. They are like those little nooks of still water, which border a rapid stream, where we may see the straw and bubble riding quietly at anchor, or slowly revolving in their mimic harbor, undisturbed by the rush of the passing current. Though many years have elapsed since I trod the drowsy shades of Sleepy Hollow, yet I question whether I should not still find the same trees and the same families vegetating in its sheltered bosom.

In this by-place of nature there abode, in a remote period of American history, that is to say, some thirty years since,[1] a worthy wight of the name of Ichabod Crane, who sojourned, or, as he expressed it, "tarried," in Sleepy Hollow, for the purpose of instructing the children of the vicinity. He was a native of Connecticut, a State which supplies the Union with pioneers for the mind as well as for the forest, and sends forth yearly its legions of frontier woodmen and country school-masters. The cognomen of Crane was not inapplicable to his person. He was tall, but exceedingly lank, with narrow shoulders, long arms and legs, hands that dangled a mile out of his sleeves, feet that might have served for shovels, and his whole frame most loosely hung together. His head was small, and flat at top, with huge ears, large green glassy eyes, and a long snipe nose, so that it looked like a weather-cock perched upon his spindle neck, to tell which way the wind blew. To see him striding along the profile of a hill on a windy day, with his clothes bagging and fluttering about him, one might have mistaken him for the genius of famine descending upon the earth, or some scarecrow eloped from a cornfield.

His school-house was a low building of one large room, rudely constructed of logs ; the windows partly glazed, and

---

[1] This story was probably written in 1818.

partly patched with leaves of copy-books. It was most in-
geniously secured at vacant hours, by a withe twisted in the
handle of the door, and stakes set against the window shutters;
so that though a thief might get in with perfect ease, he would
find some embarrassment in getting out;—an idea most probably borrowed by the architect, Yost Van Houten, from the
mystery of an eelpot. The school-house stood in a rather
lonely but pleasant situation, just at the foot of a woody hill,
with a brook running close by, and a formidable birch-tree
growing at one end of it. From hence the low murmur of
his pupils' voices, conning over their lessons, might be heard
of a drowsy summer's day, like the hum of a beehive; interrupted now and then by the authoritative voice of the master,
in the tone of menace or command; or, peradventure, by the
appalling sound of the birch, as he urged some tardy loiterer
along the flowery path of knowledge. Truth to say, he was a
conscientious man, that ever bore in mind the golden maxim,
"spare the rod and spoil the child."—Ichabod Crane's scholars
certainly were not spoiled.

I would not have it imagined, however, that he was one of
those cruel potentates of the school, who joy in the smart of
their subjects; on the contrary, he administered justice with
discrimination rather than severity; taking the burden off the
backs of the weak, and laying it on those of the strong. Your
mere puny stripling, that winced at the least flourish of the
rod, was passed by with indulgence; but the claims of justice
were satisfied by inflicting a double portion on some little,
tough, wrong-headed, broad-skirted Dutch urchin, who sulked
and swelled and grew dogged and sullen beneath the birch.
All this he called "doing his duty by their parents;" and he
never inflicted a chastisement without following it by the
assurance, so consolatory to the smarting urchin, that "he
would remember it and thank him for it the longest day he
had to live."

When school hours were over, he was even the companion

and playmate of the larger boys; and on holiday afternoons would convoy some of the smaller ones home, who happened to have pretty sisters, or good housewives for mothers, noted for the comforts of the cupboard. Indeed, it behoved him to keep on good terms with his pupils. The revenue arising from his school was small, and would have been scarcely sufficient to furnish him with daily bread, for he was a huge feeder, and though lank, had the dilating powers of an anaconda;[1] but to help out his maintenance, he was, according to country custom in those parts, boarded and lodged at the houses of the farmers, whose children he instructed. With these he lived successively a week at a time, thus going the rounds of the neighborhood, with all his worldly effects tied up in a cotton handkerchief.

That all this might not be too onerous on the purses of his rustic patrons, who are apt to consider the costs of schooling a grievous burden, and schoolmasters as mere drones, he had various ways of rendering himself both useful and agreeable. He assisted the farmers occasionally in the lighter labors of their farms; helped to make hay; mended the fences; took the horses to water; drove the cows from pasture; and cut wood for the winter fire. He laid aside, too, all the dominant dignity and absolute sway, with which he lorded it in his little empire, the school, and became wonderfully gentle and ingratiating. He found favor in the eyes of the mothers by petting the children, particularly the youngest; and like the lion bold, which whilome so magnanimously the lamb did hold,[2] he would sit with a child on one knee, and rock a cradle with his foot for whole hours together.

In addition to his other vocations, he was the singing-master of the neighborhood, and picked up many bright shillings by instructing the young folks in psalmody. It was a matter of

[1] a species of large snake.

[2] The reference is to the famous old New England primer, which, at the letter L, has the verse :

" The Lion bold
The Lamb doth hold."

no little vanity to him on Sundays, to take his station in front
of the church gallery, with a band of chosen singers ; where,
in his own mind, he completely carried away the palm from
the parson.   Certain it is, his voice resounded far above all
the rest of the congregation, and there are peculiar quavers
still to be heard in that church, and which may even be heard
half a mile off, quite to the opposite side of the mill-pond, on
a still Sunday morning, which are said to be legitimately
descended from the nose of Ichabod Crane.   Thus, by divers
little make-shifts, in that ingenious way which is commonly
denominated "by hook and by crook," the worthy pedagogue
got on tolerably enough, and was thought, by all who understood nothing of the labor of head-work, to have a wonderful
easy life of it.

The schoolmaster is generally a man of some importance
in the female circle of a rural neighborhood ; being considered
a kind of idle gentleman-like personage, of vastly superior
taste and accomplishments to the rough country swains, and,
indeed, inferior in learning only to the parson.   His appearance, therefore, is apt to occasion some little stir at the tea-
table of a farm-house, and the addition of a supernumerary
dish of cakes or sweetmeats, or, peradventure, the parade of
a silver tea-pot.   Our man of letters, therefore, was peculiarly
happy in the smiles of all the country damsels.   How he
would figure among them in the churchyard between services
on Sundays! gathering grapes for them from the wild vines
that overrun the surrounding trees ; reciting for their amusement all the epitaphs on the tombstones ; or sauntering, with
a whole bevy of them, along the banks of the adjacent mill-
pond ; while the most bashful country bumpkins hung sheep-
ishly back, envying his superior elegance and address.

From his half itinerant life, also, he was a kind of travel-
ling gazette,[1] carrying the whole budget of local gossip from
house to house ; so that his appearance was always greeted

---

[1] a word for newspaper, more common in Irving's day than ours.

with satisfaction. He was, moreover, esteemed by the women as a man of great erudition, for he had read several books quite through, and was a perfect master of Cotton Mather's History of New England Witchcraft,[1] in which, by the way, he most firmly and potently believed.

He was, in fact, an odd mixture of small shrewdness and simple credulity. His appetite for the marvellous, and his powers of digesting it, were equally extraordinary; and both had been increased by his residence in this spell-bound region. No tale was too gross or monstrous for his capacious swallow. It was often his delight, after his school was dismissed in the afternoon, to stretch himself on the rich bed of clover, bordering the little brook that whimpered by his school-house, and there con over old Mather's direful tales, until the gathering dusk of evening made the printed page a mere mist before his eyes. Then, as he wended his way, by swamp and stream and awful woodland, to the farm-house where he happened to be quartered, every sound of nature, at that witching hour, fluttered his excited imagination: the moan of the whip-poor-will * from the hill-side; the boding cry of the tree-toad, that harbinger of storm; the dreary hooting of the screech-owl; or the sudden rustling in the thicket, of birds frightened from their roost. The fire-flies, too, which sparkled most vividly in the darkest places, now and then startled him, as one of uncommon brightness would stream across his path; and if, by chance, a huge blockhead of a beetle came winging his blundering flight against him, the poor varlet was ready to give up the ghost, with the idea that he was struck with a witch's token. His only resource on such occasions, either to drown thought, or drive away evil spirits, was to sing psalm tunes;—and the good people of Sleepy Hollow, as they sat by their doors of an evening, were often filled with

---

[1] Cotton Mather was a famous Boston clergyman (1663-1738). He was the historian of his day. Like others of his time, he believed firmly in witchcraft.

* The whip-poor-will is a bird which is only heard at night. It receives its name from its note, which is thought to resemble those words.—*Author's Note.*

awe, at hearing his nasal melody, "in linked sweetness long
drawn out," floating from the distant hill, or along the dusky
road.

Another of his sources of fearful pleasure was, to pass
long winter evenings with the old Dutch wives, as they sat
spinning by the fire, with a row of apples roasting and sput-
tering along the hearth, and listen to their marvellous tales
of ghosts, and goblins, and haunted fields and haunted brooks,
and haunted bridges and haunted houses, and particularly of
the headless horseman, or galloping Hessian of the Hollow,
as they sometimes called him. He would delight them
equally by his anecdotes of witchcraft, and of the direful
omens and portentous sights and sounds in the air, which prevailed in the earlier times of Connecticut; and would frighten
them wofully with speculations upon comets and shooting
stars, and with the alarming fact that the world did absolutely
turn round, and that they were half the time topsy-turvy!

But if there was a pleasure in all this, while snugly cud-
dling in the chimney corner of a chamber that was all of a
ruddy glow from the crackling wood fire, and where, of course,
no spectre dared to show its face, it was dearly purchased by
the terrors of his subsequent walk homewards. What fearful shapes and shadows beset his path, amidst the dim and
ghastly glare of a snowy night!—With what wistful look did
he eye every trembling ray of light streaming across the
waste fields from some distant window!—How often was he
appalled by some shrub covered with snow, which like a
sheeted spectre beset his very path!—How often did he
shrink with curdling awe at the sound of his own steps on
the frosty crust beneath his feet; and dread to look over his
shoulder, lest he should behold some uncouth being tramping
close behind him!—and how often was he thrown into complete dismay by some rushing blast, howling among the trees,
in the idea that it was the galloping Hessian on one of his
nightly scourings!

8

All these, however, were mere terrors of the night, phantoms of the mind, that walk in darkness : and though he had seen many spectres in his time, and been more than once beset by Satan in divers shapes, in his lonely perambulations, yet daylight put an end to all these evils ; and he would have passed a pleasant life of it, in despite of the Devil and all his works, if his path had not been crossed by a being that causes more perplexity to mortal man, than ghosts, goblins, and the whole race of witches put together ; and that was—a woman.

Among the musical disciples who assembled, one evening in each week, to receive his instructions in psalmody, was Katrina Van Tassel, the daughter and only child of a substantial Dutch farmer. She was a blooming lass of fresh eighteen ; plump as a partridge ; ripe and melting and rosy-cheeked as one of her father's peaches, and universally famed, not merely for her beauty, but her vast expectations. She was withal a little of a coquette, as might be perceived even in her dress, which was a mixture of ancient and modern fashions, as most suited to set off her charms. She wore the ornaments of pure yellow gold, which her great-great-grandmother had brought over from Saardam ;[1] the tempting stomacher of the olden time, and withal a provokingly short petticoat, to display the prettiest foot and ankle in the country round.

Ichabod Crane had a soft and foolish heart towards the sex ; and it is not to be wondered at, that so tempting a morsel soon found favor in his eyes, more especially after he had visited her in her paternal mansion. Old Baltus Van Tassel[2] was a perfect picture of a thriving, contented, liberal-hearted farmer. He seldom, it is true, sent either his eyes or his thoughts beyond the boundaries of his own farm ; but within these, everything was snug, happy and well-conditioned. He was satisfied with his wealth, but not proud of it ; and

<hr>

[1] In Holland, near Amsterdam.   [2] See p. 64.

piqued himself upon the hearty abundance, rather than the style in which he lived.   His stronghold was situated on the banks of the Hudson, in one of those green, sheltered, fertile nooks, in which the Dutch farmers are so fond of nestling. A great elm-tree spread its broad branches over it ; at the foot of which bubbled up a spring of the softest and sweetest water, in a little well, formed of a barrel ; and then stole sparkling away through the grass, to a neighboring brook, that babbled along among alders and dwarf willows.   Hard by the farm-house was a vast barn, that might have served for a church ; every window and crevice of which seemed bursting forth with the treasures of the farm ; the flail was busily resounding within it from morning to night ; swallows and martins skimmed twittering about the eaves ; and rows of pigeons, some with one eye turned up, as if watching the weather, some with their heads under their wings, or buried in their bosoms, and others, swelling, and cooing, and bowing about their dames, were enjoying the sunshine on the roof. Sleek unwieldy porkers were grunting in the repose and abundance of their pens, from whence sallied forth, now and then, troops of sucking pigs, as if to snuff the air.   A stately squadron of snowy geese were riding in an adjoining pond, convoying whole fleets of ducks ; regiments of turkeys were gobbling through the farm-yard, and guinea-fowls fretting about it like ill-tempered housewives, with their peevish, discontented cry. Before the barn door strutted the gallant cock, that pattern of a husband, a warrior, and a fine gentleman ; clapping his burnished wings and crowing in the pride and gladness of his heart—sometimes tearing up the earth with his feet, and then generously calling his ever-hungry family of wives and children to enjoy the rich morsel which he had discovered.

The pedagogue's mouth watered, as he looked upon this sumptuous promise of luxurious winter fare.   In his devouring mind's eye, he pictured to himself every roasting pig running about, with a pudding in its belly, and an apple in its mouth ;

the pigeons were snugly put to bed in a comfortable pie, and tucked in with a coverlet of crust; the geese were swimming in their own gravy; and the ducks pairing cosily in dishes, like snug married couples, with a decent competency of onion sauce. In the porkers he saw carved out the future sleek side of bacon, and juicy relishing ham; not a turkey, but he beheld daintily trussed up, with its gizzard under its wing, and, peradventure, a necklace of savory sausages; and even bright chanticleer himself lay sprawling on his back, in a side dish, with uplifted claws, as if craving that quarter which his chivalrous spirit disdained to ask while living.

As the enraptured Ichabod fancied all this, and as he rolled his great green eyes over the fat meadow lands, the rich fields of wheat, of rye, of buckwheat, and Indian corn, and the orchards burdened with ruddy fruit, which surrounded the warm tenement of Van Tassel, his heart yearned after the damsel who was to inherit these domains, and his imagination expanded with the idea, how they might be readily turned into cash, and the money invested in immense tracts of wild land, and shingle palaces in the wilderness. Nay. his busy fancy already realized his hopes, and presented to him the blooming Katrina, with a whole family of children mounted on the top of a wagon loaded with household trumpery, with pots and kettles dangling beneath; and he beheld himself bestriding a pacing mare, with a colt at her heels, setting out for Kentucky, Tennessee [1]—or the Lord knows where!

When he entered the house, the conquest of his heart was complete. It was one of those spacious farm-houses, with high-ridged, but lowly-sloping roofs, built in the style handed down from the first Dutch settlers. The low projecting eaves forming a piazza along the front, capable of being

---

[1] Kentucky and Tennessee were then the objects of emigration, just as the more Western States later. It was a pet idea of Irving's that the New Englanders were always emigrating. In "Knickerbocker," bk. iii., ch. viii., he says that they never get half settled before they wish to emigrate again.

closed up in bad weather. Under this were hung flails, har-
ness, various utensils of husbandry, and nets for fishing in
the neighboring river. Benches were built along the sides
for summer use ; and a great spinning-wheel at one end, and
a churn at the other, showed the various uses to which this
important porch might be devoted. From this piazza the
wonderful Ichabod entered the hall, which formed the centre
of the mansion, and the place of usual residence. Here,
rows of resplendent pewter, ranged on a long dresser, dazzled
his eyes. In one corner stood a huge bag of wool, ready to
be spun ; in another, a quantity of linsey-woolsey just from
the loom ; ears of Indian corn, and strings of dried apples
and peaches, hung in gay festoons along the walls, mingled
with the gaud of red peppers ; and a door left ajar, gave him
a peep into the best parlor, where the claw-footed chairs, and
dark mahogany tables, shone like mirrors ; andirons, with
their accompanying shovel and tongs, glistened from their
covert of asparagus tops ; mock-oranges and conch shells
decorated the mantelpiece ; strings of various colored birds'
eggs were suspended above it ; a great ostrich egg was hung
from the centre of the room, and a corner cupboard, knowingly
left open, displayed immense treasures of old silver and well-
mended china.

From the moment Ichabod laid his eyes upon these regions of delight, the peace of his mind was at an end, and
his only study was how to gain the affections of the peerless
daughter of Van Tassel. In this enterprise, however, he
had more real difficulties than generally fell to the lot of a
knight-errant of yore, who seldom had anything but giants,
enchanters, fiery dragons, and such like easily conquered adversaries, to contend with ; and had to make his way merely
through gates of iron and brass, and walls of adamant to the
castle-keep, where the lady of his heart was confined ; all
which he achieved as easily as a man would carve his way to
the centre of a Christmas pie, and then the lady gave him

her hand as a matter of course. Ichabod, on the contrary,
had to win his way to the heart of a country coquette, beset
with a labyrinth of whims and caprices, which were forever
presenting new difficulties and impediments, and he had to
encounter a host of fearful adversaries of real flesh and blood,
the numerous rustic admirers, who beset every portal to her
heart ; keeping a watchful and angry eye upon each other,
but ready to fly out in the common cause against any new
competitor.

Among these, the most formidable was a burly, roaring,
roystering blade, of the name of Abraham, or according to
the Dutch abbreviation, Brom Van Brunt, the hero of the
country round, which rung with his feats of strength and
hardihood. He was broad-shouldered and double-jointed,
with short curly black hair, and a bluff, but not unpleasant
countenance, having a mingled air of fun and arrogance.
From his Herculean frame and great powers of limb, he had
received the nickname of BROM BONES, by which he was universally known. He was famed for great knowledge and
skill in horsemanship, being as dexterous on horseback as a
Tartar.[1] He was foremost at all races and cock-fights, and
with the ascendancy which bodily strength always acquires in
rustic life, was the umpire in all disputes, setting his hat on
one side, and giving his decisions with an air and tone that
admitted of no gainsay or appeal. He was always ready for
either a fight or a frolic ; had more mischief than ill-will in
his composition ; and with all his overbearing roughness,
there was a strong dash of waggish good humor at bottom.
He had three or four boon companions of his own stamp,
who regarded him as their model, and at the head of whom
he scoured the country, attending every scene of feud or
merriment for miles around. In cold weather, he was distinguished by a fur cap, surmounted with a flaunting fox's tail ;

[1] The Tartars are wandering peoples of Asia. The Cossacks (some of whom live
on the river Don) are famous horsemen.

and when the folks at a country gathering descried this well-known crest at a distance, whisking about among a squad of hard riders, they always stood by for a squall. Sometimes his crew would be heard dashing along past the farm-houses at midnight, with whoop and halloo, like a troop of Don Cossacks, and the old dames, startled out of their sleep, would listen for a moment till the hurry-scurry had clattered by, and then exclaim, " Ay, there goes Brom Bones and his gang !" The neighbors looked upon him with a mixture of awe, admiration, and good-will ; and when any madcap prank, or rustic brawl occurred in the vicinity, always shook their heads, and warranted Brom Bones was at the bottom of it.

This rantipole¹ hero had for some time singled out the blooming Katrina for the object of his uncouth gallantries, and though his amorous toyings were something like the gentle caresses and endearments of a bear, yet it was whispered that she did not altogether discourage his hopes. Certain it is, his advances were signals for rival candidates to retire, who felt no inclination to cross a lion in his amours ; insomuch, that when his horse was seen tied to Van Tassel's palings, on a Sunday night, a sure sign that his master was courting, or, as it is termed, " sparking," within, all other suitors passed by in despair, and carried the war into other quarters.

Such was the formidable rival with whom Ichabod Crane had to contend, and considering all things, a stouter man than he would have shrunk from the competition, and a wiser man would have despaired. He had, however, a happy mixture of pliability and perseverance in his nature ; he was in form and spirit like a supple-jack ²—yielding, but tough ; though he bent, he never broke ; and though he bowed beneath the slightest pressure, yet, the moment it was away—jerk !—he was as erect, and carried his head as high as ever.

To have taken the field openly against his rival, would

---

¹ wild, roving, rakish.   ² a strong, pliant cane.

have been madness; for he was not a man to be thwarted in his amours, any more than that stormy lover, Achilles.[1] Ichabod, therefore, made his advances in a quiet and gently-insinuating manner. Under cover of his character of singing-master, he made frequent visits at the farm-house; not that he had anything to apprehend from the meddlesome interference of parents, which is so often a stumbling-block in the path of lovers. Balt Van Tassel was an easy indulgent soul; he loved his daughter better even than his pipe, and like a reasonable man, and an excellent father, let her have her way in everything. His notable little wife, too, had enough to do to attend to her housekeeping and manage the poultry; for, as she sagely observed, ducks and geese are foolish things, and must be looked after, but girls can take care of themselves. Thus, while the busy dame bustled about the house, or plied her spinning-wheel at one end of the piazza, honest Balt would sit smoking his evening pipe at the other, watching the achievements of a little wooden warrior, who, armed with a sword in each hand, was most valiantly fighting the wind on the pinnacle of the barn. In the mean time, Ichabod would carry on his suit with the daughter by the side of the spring under the great elm, or sauntering along in the twilight, that hour so favorable to the lover's eloquence.

I profess not to know how women's hearts are wooed and won. To me they have always been matters of riddle and admiration. Some seem to have but one vulnerable point, or door of access; while others have a thousand avenues, and may be captured in a thousand different ways. It is a great triumph of skill to gain the former, but a still greater proof of generalship to maintain possession of the latter, for a man must battle for his fortress at every door and window. He that wins a thousand common hearts, is therefore entitled to some renown; but he who keeps undisputed sway over the heart of a coquette, is indeed a hero. Certain it is, this was

<hr />

[1] the great hero of the Greeks in the Trojan war.

not the case with the redoubtable Brom Bones ; and from the moment Ichabod Crane made his advances, the interests of the former evidently declined : his horse was no longer seen tied at the palings on Sunday nights, and a deadly feud gradually arose between him and the preceptor of Sleepy Hollow.

Brom, who had a degree of rough chivalry in his nature, would fain have carried matters to open warfare, and settled their pretensions to the lady, according to the mode of those most concise and simple reasoners, the knights errant of yore —by single combat ; but Ichabod was too conscious of the superior might of his adversary to enter the lists against him ; he had overheard the boast of Bones, that he would "double the schoolmaster up, and put him on a shelf;" and he was too wary to give him an opportunity. There was something extremely provoking in this obstinately pacific system ; it left Brom no alternative but to draw upon the funds of rustic waggery in his disposition, and to play off boorish practical jokes upon his rival. Ichabod became the object of whimsical persecution to Bones, and his gang of rough riders. They harried his hitherto peaceful domains ; smoked out his singing-school, by stopping up the chimney ; broke into the schoolhouse at night, in spite of its formidable fastenings of withe and window stakes, and turned everything topsy-turvy ; so that the poor schoolmaster began to think all the witches in the country held their meetings there. But what was still more annoying, Brom took all opportunities of turning him into ridicule in presence of his mistress, and had a scoundrel dog whom he taught to whine in the most ludicrous manner, and introduced as a rival of Ichabod's, to instruct her in psalmody.

In this way, matters went on for some time, without producing any material effect on the relative situations of the contending powers. On a fine autumnal afternoon, Ichabod, in pensive mood, sat enthroned on the lofty stool from whence he usually watched all the concerns of his literary realm. In his hand he swayed a ferule, that sceptre of despotic power ;

the birch of justice reposed on three nails, behind the throne, a constant terror to evil doers; while on the desk before him might be seen sundry contraband articles and prohibited weapons, detected upon the persons of idle urchins; such as half-munched apples, popguns, whirligigs, fly-cages, and whole legions of rampant little paper game-cocks. Apparently there had been some appalling act of justice recently inflicted, for his scholars were all busily intent upon their books, or slyly whispering behind them with one eye kept upon the master; and a kind of buzzing stillness reigned throughout the school-room. It was suddenly interrupted by the appearance of a negro in tow-cloth jacket and trowsers, a round crowned fragment of a hat, like the cap of Mercury,[1] and mounted on the back of a ragged, wild, half-broken colt, which he managed with a rope by way of halter. He came clattering up to the school-door with an invitation to Ichabod to attend a merry-making, or "quilting-frolic,"[2] to be held that evening at Mynheer Van Tassel's; and having delivered his message with that air of importance, and effort at fine language, which a negro is apt to display on petty embassies of the kind, he dashed over the brook, and was seen scampering away up the Hollow, full of the importance and hurry of his mission.

All was now bustle and hubbub in the late quiet school-room. The scholars were hurried through their lessons, without stopping at trifles; those who were nimble, skipped over half with impunity, and those who were tardy, had a smart application now and then in the rear, to quicken their speed, or help them over a tall word. Books were flung aside, without being put away on the shelves; inkstands were overturned, benches thrown down, and the whole school was turned loose an hour before the usual time; bursting forth like a legion of

[1] the messenger of the gods in the classic mythology. He wears a low-crowned, broad-brimmed flattish hat, familiar to us in the statuettes and busts of the Flying Mercury.

[2] The making of a quilt was the occasion for the whole neighborhood to gather to help; after the work there was plenty of good entertainment.

young imps, yelping and racketing about the green, in joy at their early emancipation.

The gallant Ichabod now spent at least an extra half-hour at his toilet, brushing and furbishing up his best, and indeed only suit of rusty black, and arranging his looks by a bit of broken looking-glass, that hung up in the school-house. That he might make his appearance before his mistress in the true style of a cavalier, he borrowed a horse from the farmer with whom he was domiciliated, a choleric old Dutchman, of the name of Hans Van Ripper, and thus gallantly mounted, issued forth like a knight-errant in quest of adventures. But it is meet I should, in the true spirit of romantic story, give some account of the looks and equipments of my hero and his steed. The animal he bestrode was a broken-down plough-horse, that had outlived almost everything but his viciousness. He was gaunt and shagged, with a ewe neck [1] and a head like a hammer ; his rusty mane and tail were tangled and knotted with burrs ; one eye had lost its pupil, and was glaring and spectral, but the other had the gleam of a genuine devil in it. Still he must have had fire and mettle in his day, if we may judge from his name, which was Gunpowder. He had, in fact, been a favorite steed of his master's, the choleric Van Ripper, who was a furious rider, and had infused, very probably, some of his own spirit into the animal ; for, old and broken-down as he looked, there was more of the lurking devil in him than in any young filly in the country.

Ichabod was a suitable figure for such a steed. He rode with short stirrups, which brought his knees nearly up to the pommel of the saddle ; his sharp elbows stuck out like grass-hoppers' ; he carried his whip perpendicularly in his hand, like a sceptre, and as the horse jogged on, the motion of his arms was not unlike the flapping of a pair of wings. A small wool hat rested on the top of his nose, for so his scanty strip of forehead might be called, and the skirts of his black coat

_____
[1] a thin, hollow neck.

fluttered out almost to the horse's tail.   Such was the appearance of Ichabod and his steed as they shambled out of the gate of Hans Van Ripper, and it was altogether such an apparition as is seldom to be met with in broad daylight.

It was, as I have said, a fine autumnal day; the sky was clear and serene, and nature wore that rich and golden livery which we always associate with the idea of abundance.   The forests had put on their sober brown and yellow, while some trees of the tenderer kind had been nipped by the frosts into brilliant dyes of orange, purple, and scarlet.   Streaming files of wild ducks began to make their appearance high in the air; the bark of the squirrel might be heard from the groves of beech and hickory-nuts, and the pensive whistle of the quail at intervals from the neighboring stubble field.

The small birds were taking their farewell banquets.   In the fulness of their revelry, they fluttered, chirping and frolicking, from bush to bush, and tree to tree, capricious from the very profusion and variety around them.   There was the honest cockrobin, the favorite game of stripling sportsmen, with its loud querulous note, and the twittering blackbirds flying in sable clouds; and the golden-winged woodpecker, with his crimson crest, his broad black gorget, and splendid plumage; and the cedar-bird, with its red-tipt wings and yellow-tipt tail and its little monteiro cap[1] of feathers; and the blue jay, that noisy coxcomb, in his gay light blue coat and white underclothes, screaming and chattering, nodding, and bobbing, and bowing, and pretending to be on good terms with every songster of the grove.

As Ichabod jogged slowly on his way, his eye, ever open to every symptom of culinary abundance, ranged with delight over the treasures of jolly autumn.   On all sides he beheld vast store of apples, some hanging in oppressive opulence on the trees; some gathered into baskets and barrels for the market; others heaped up in rich piles for the cider-press.

[1] a round cap, with flaps which covered the sides of the face.

Farther on he beheld great fields of Indian corn, with its golden ears peeping from their leafy coverts, and holding out the promise of cakes and hasty-pudding; and the yellow pumpkins lying beneath them, turning up their fair round bellies to the sun, and giving ample prospects of the most luxurious of pies; and anon he passed the fragrant buckwheat fields breathing the odor of the beehive, and as he beheld them, soft anticipations stole over his mind of dainty slap-jacks, well-buttered, and garnished with honey or treacle, by the delicate little dimpled hand of Katrina Van Tassel.

Thus feeding his mind with many sweet thoughts and "sugared suppositions," he journeyed along the sides of a range of hills which look out upon some of the goodliest scenes of the mighty Hudson. The sun gradually wheeled his broad disk down in the west. The wide bosom of the Tappaan Zee lay motionless and glassy, excepting that here and there a gentle undulation waved and prolonged the blue shadow of the distant mountain. A few amber clouds floated in the sky, without a breath of air to move them. The horizon was of a fine golden tint, changing gradually into a pure apple green,[1] and from that into the deep blue of the mid-heaven. A slanting ray lingered on the woody crests of the precipices that overhung some parts of the river, giving greater depth to the dark gray and purple of their rocky sides. A sloop was loitering in the distance, dropping slowly down with the tide, her sail hanging uselessly against the mast; and as the reflection of the sky gleamed along the still water, it seemed as if the vessel was suspended in the air.

It was toward evening that Ichabod arrived at the castle of the Heer Van Tassel, which he found thronged with the pride and flower of the adjacent country. Old farmers, a spare leathern-faced race, in homespun coats and breeches, blue stockings, huge shoes, and magnificent pewter buckles. Their brisk, withered little dames, in close crimped caps, long-

---

[1] Notice the green in the sky some fine sunset in the summer.

waisted gowns, homespun petticoats, with scissors and pin-cushions, and gay calico pockets, hanging on the outside. Buxom lasses, almost as antiquated as their mothers, excepting where a straw hat, a fine ribbon, or perhaps a white frock, gave symptoms of city innovations. The sons, in short square skirted coats, with rows of stupendous brass buttons, and their hair generally queued [1] in the fashion of the times, especially if they could procure an eelskin for the purpose, it being esteemed throughout the country, as a potent nourisher and strengthener of the hair.

Brom Bones, however, was the hero of the scene, having come to the gathering on his favorite steed, Daredevil, a creature, like himself, full of mettle and mischief, and which no one but himself could manage. He was, in fact, noted for preferring vicious animals, given to all kinds of tricks which kept the rider in constant risk of his neck, for he held a tractable well-broken horse as unworthy of a lad of spirit.

Fain would I pause to dwell upon the world of charms that burst upon the enraptured gaze of my hero, as he entered the state parlor of Van Tassel's mansion. Not those of the bevy of buxom lasses, with their luxurious display of red and white; but the ample charms of a genuine Dutch country tea-table, in the sumptuous time of autumn. Such heaped up platters of cakes of various and almost indescribable kinds, known only to experienced Dutch housewives! There was the doughty dough-nut, the tender olykoek, and the crisp and crumbling cruller; sweet cakes and short cakes, ginger cakes and honey cakes, and the whole family of cakes. And then there were apple pies, and peach pies, and pumpkin pies; besides slices of ham and smoked beef; and moreover delectable dishes of preserved plums, and peaches, and pears, and quinces; not to mention broiled shad and roasted chickens; together with bowls of milk and cream, all mingled higgledy-piggledy, pretty

---

[1] put into a queue or pigtail.

much as I have enumerated them, with the motherly tea-pot sending up its clouds of vapor from the midst—Heaven bless the mark! I want breath and time to discuss this banquet as it deserves, and am too eager to get on with my story. Happily, Ichabod Crane was not in so great a hurry as his historian, but did ample justice to every dainty.

He was a kind and thankful creature, whose heart dilated in proportion as his skin was filled with good cheer, and whose spirits rose with eating, as some men's do with drink. He could not help, too, rolling his large eyes round him as he ate, and chuckling with the possibility that he might one day be lord of all this scene of almost unimaginable luxury and splendor. Then, he thought, how soon he'd turn his back upon the old school-house; snap his fingers in the face of Hans Van Ripper, and every other niggardly patron, and kick any itinerant pedagogue out of doors that should dare to call him comrade!

Old Baltus Van Tassel moved about among his guests with a face dilated with content and good-humor, round and jolly as the harvest moon. His hospitable attentions were brief, but expressive, being confined to a shake of the hand, a slap on the shoulder, a loud laugh, and a pressing invitation to "fall to, and help themselves."

And now the sound of the music from the common room, or hall, summoned to the dance. The musician was an old gray-headed negro, who had been the itinerant orchestra of the neighborhood for more than half a century. His instrument was as old and battered as himself. The greater part of the time he scraped away on two or three strings, accompanying every movement of the bow with a motion of the head; bowing almost to the ground, and stamping with his foot whenever a fresh couple were to start.

Ichabod prided himself upon his dancing as much as upon his vocal powers. Not a limb, not a fibre about him was idle; and to have seen his loosely hung frame in full motion, and clattering about the room, you would have thought St. Vitus [1] himself, that blessed patron of the dance, was figuring before you in person. He was the admiration of all the negroes; who, having gathered, of all ages and sizes, from the farm and the neighborhood, stood forming a pyramid of shining black faces at every door and window; gazing with delight at the scene; rolling their white eye-balls, and showing grinning rows of ivory from ear to ear. How could the flogger of urchins be otherwise than animated and joyous? the lady of his heart was his partner in the dance, and smiling graciously in reply to all his amorous oglings; while Brom Bones, sorely smitten with love and jealousy, sat brooding by himself in one corner.

When the dance was at an end, Ichabod was attracted to a knot of the sager folks, who, with Old Van Tassel, sat smoking at one end of the piazza, gossiping over former times, and drawling out long stories about the war.

This neighborhood, at the time of which I am speaking, was one of those highly favored places which abound with chronicle and great men. The British and American line had run near it during the war; it had, therefore, been the scene of marauding, and infested with refugees, Cowboys,[2] and all kind of border chivalry. Just sufficient time had elapsed to enable each story-teller to dress up his tale with a little becoming fiction, and, in the indistinctness of his recollection, to make himself the hero of every exploit.

There was the story of Doffue Martling, a large blue-bearded Dutchman, who had nearly taken a British frigate with an old iron nine-pounder from a mud breastwork, only that his gun burst at the sixth discharge. And there was an old gentleman who shall be nameless, being too rich a mynheer

---

[1] In some parts of Germany it was believed that health could be restored by dancing in the Chapel of St. Vitus. "St. Vitus' dance" is the name given to a nervous disorder.

[2] See "Wolfert's Roost," p. 66.

to be lightly mentioned, who in the battle of Whiteplains,[1] being an excellent master of defence, parried a musket-ball with a small-sword, insomuch that he absolutely felt it whiz round the blade, and glance off at the hilt ; in proof of which he was ready at any time to show the sword, with the hilt a little bent. There were several more that had been equally great in the field, not one of whom but was persuaded that he had a considerable hand in bringing the war to a happy termination.

But all these were nothing to the tales of ghosts and apparitions that succeeded. The neighborhood is rich in legendary treasures of the kind. Local tales and superstitions thrive best in these sheltered, long-settled retreats ; but are trampled under foot, by the shifting throng that forms the population of most of our country places. Besides, there is no encouragement for ghosts in most of our villages, for they have scarcely had time to finish their first nap, and turn themselves in their graves, before their surviving friends have travelled away from the neighborhood ; so that when they turn out at night to walk their rounds, they have no acquaintance left to call upon. This is perhaps the reason why we so seldom hear of ghosts except in our long-established Dutch communities.

The immediate cause, however, of the prevalence of supernatural stories in these parts, was doubtless owing to the vicinity of Sleepy Hollow. There was a contagion in the very air that blew from that haunted region ; it breathed forth an atmosphere of dreams and fancies infecting all the land. Several of the Sleepy Hollow people were present at Van Tassel's, and, as usual, were doling out their wild and wonderful legends. Many dismal tales were told about funeral trains, and mourning cries and wailings heard and seen about the great tree where the unfortunate Major André[2] was taken, and

[1] a village about twenty miles north of New York. The battle was fought October 26, 1776.

[2] An English officer who carried messages between Benedict Arnold and the English general. He was captured by three Americans, September 23, 1780, and hanged as a spy a week later.

which stood in the neighborhood. Some mention was made also of the woman in white, that haunted the dark glen at Raven Rock, and was often heard to shriek on winter nights before a storm, having perished there in the snow. The chief part of the stories, however, turned upon the favorite spectre of Sleepy Hollow, the headless horseman, who had been heard several times of late, patrolling the country; and it is said, tethered his horse nightly among the graves in the churchyard.

The sequestered situation of this church seems always to have made it a favorite haunt of troubled spirits. It stands on a knoll, surrounded by locust-trees and lofty elms, from among which its decent, whitewashed walls shine modestly forth, like Christian purity, beaming through the shades of retirement. A gentle slope descends from it to a silver sheet of water, bordered by high trees, between which, peeps may be caught at the blue hills of the Hudson. To look upon its grass-grown yard, where the sunbeams seem to sleep so quietly, one would think that there at least the dead might rest in peace. On one side of the church extends a wide woody dell, along which raves a large brook among broken rocks and trunks of fallen trees. Over a deep black part of the stream, not far from the church, was formerly thrown a wooden bridge; the road that led to it, and the bridge itself, were thickly shaded by overhanging trees, which cast a gloom about it, even in the daytime; but occasioned a fearful darkness at night. Such was one of the favorite haunts of the headless horseman, and the place where he was most frequently encountered. The tale was told of old Brouwer, a most heretical disbeliever in ghosts, how he met the horseman returning from his foray into Sleepy Hollow, and was obliged to get up behind him; how they galloped over bush and brake, over hill and swamp, until they reached the bridge; when the horseman suddenly turned into a skeleton, threw old Brouwer into the brook, and sprang away over the tree tops with a clap of thunder.

This story was immediately matched by a thrice marvellous

adventure of Brom Bones, who made light of the galloping
Hessian as an arrant jockey.   He affirmed, that on returning
one night from the neighboring village of Sing-Sing, he had
been overtaken by this midnight trooper ; that he had offered
to race with him for a bowl of punch, and should have won it
too, for Daredevil beat the goblin horse all hollow, but just as
they came to the church bridge, the Hessian bolted, and van-
ished in a flash of fire.[1]

All these tales, told in that drowsy undertone with which
men talk in the dark, the countenances of the listeners only
now and then receiving a casual gleam from the glare of a
pipe, sunk deep in the mind of Ichabod.   He repaid them in
kind with large extracts from his invaluable author, Cotton
Mather, and added many marvellous events that had taken
place in his native State of Connecticut, and fearful sights
which he had seen in his nightly walks about Sleepy Hollow.

The revel now gradually broke up.   The old farmers gathered together their families in their wagons, and were heard
for some time rattling along the hollow roads, and over the
distant hills.   Some of the damsels mounted on pillions[2]
behind their favorite swains, and their light-hearted laughter,
mingling with the clatter of hoofs, echoed along the silent
woodlands, sounding fainter and fainter, until they gradually
died away—and the late scene of noise and frolic was all silent
and deserted.   Ichabod only lingered behind, according to the
custom of country lovers, to have a tête-à-tête with the heiress ; fully convinced that he was now on the high road to success.   What passed at this interview I will not pretend to say,
for in fact I do not know.   Something, however, I fear me,
must have gone wrong, for he certainly sallied forth, after no
very great interval, with an air quite desolate and chapfallen—
Oh, these women ! these women !   Could that girl have been
playing off any of her coquettish tricks ?—Was her encourage-

[1] This tale was that which originally gave
Irving the hint for the story. See p. 20.

[2] small seats whereon women could ride
on horseback, behind the men.

ment of the poor pedagogue all a mere sham to secure her conquest of his rival ?—Heaven only knows, not I !—Let it suffice to say, Ichabod stole forth with the air of one who had
been sacking a hen-roost, rather than a fair lady's heart.
Without looking to the right or left to notice the scene of
rural wealth, on which he had so often gloated, he went
straight to the stable, and with several hearty cuffs and kicks,
roused his steed most uncourteously from the comfortable
quarters in which he was soundly sleeping, dreaming of
mountains of corn and oats, and whole valleys of timothy and
clover.

It was the very witching time of night that Ichabod, heavy-
hearted and crest-fallen, pursued his travel homewards, along
the sides of the lofty hills which rise above Tarry Town, and
which he had traversed so cheerily in the afternoon.   The
hour was as dismal as himself.   Far below him the Tappaan
Zee spread its dusky and indistinct waste of waters, with here
and there the tall mast of a sloop, riding quietly at anchor
under the land.   In the dead hush of midnight, he could even
hear the barking of the watch-dog from the opposite shore of
the Hudson ; but it was so vague and faint as only to give an
idea of his distance from this faithful companion of man.
Now and then, too, the long-drawn crowing of a cock, acci-
dentally awakened, would sound far, far off, from some farm-
house away among the hills—but it was like a dreaming sound
in his ear.   No sign of life occurred near him, but occasionally
the melancholy chirp of a cricket, or perhaps the guttural
twang of a bull-frog from a neighboring marsh, as if sleeping
uncomfortably, and turning suddenly in his bed.

All the stories of ghosts and goblins that he had heard in
the afternoon, now came crowding upon his recollection.   The
night grew darker and darker ; the stars seemed to sink deeper
in the sky, and driving clouds occasionally hid them from his
sight.   He had never felt so lonely and dismal.   He was,
moreover, approaching the very place where many of the scenes

of the ghost stories had been laid. In the centre of the road stood an enormous tulip-tree, which towered like a giant above all the other trees of the neighborhood, and formed a kind of landmark. Its limbs were gnarled and fantastic, large enough to form trunks for ordinary trees, twisting down almost to the earth, and rising again into the air. It was connected with the tragical story of the unfortunate André, who had been taken prisoner hard by ; and was universally known by the name of Major André's tree. The common people regarded it with a mixture of respect and superstition, partly out of sympathy for the fate of its ill-starred namesake, and partly from the tales of strange sights, and doleful lamentations, told concerning it.

As Ichabod approached this fearful tree, he began to whistle ; he thought his whistle was answered : it was but a blast sweeping sharply through the dry branches. As he approached a little nearer, he thought he saw something white, hanging in the midst of the tree : he paused, and ceased whistling ; but on looking more narrowly, perceived that it was a place where the tree had been scathed by lightning, and the white wood laid bare. Suddenly he heard a groan—his teeth chattered, and his knees smote against the saddle : it was but the rubbing of one huge bough upon another, as they were swayed about by the breeze. He passed the tree in safety, but new perils lay before him.

About two hundred yards from the tree, a small brook crossed the road, and ran into a marshy and thickly-wooded glen, known by the name of Wiley's Swamp. A few rough logs, laid side by side, served for a bridge over this stream. On that side of the road where the brook entered the wood, a group of oaks and chestnuts, matted thick with wild grape-vines, threw a cavernous gloom over it. To pass this bridge, was the severest trial. It was at this identical spot that the unfortunate André was captured, and under the covert of those chestnuts and vines were the sturdy yeomen concealed

who surprised him. This has ever since been considered a
haunted stream, and fearful are the feelings of a school-boy
who has to pass it alone after dark.

As he approached the stream, his heart began to thump;
he summoned up, however, all his resolution, gave his horse
half a score of kicks in the ribs, and attempted to dash briskly
across the bridge; but instead of starting forward, the per-
verse old animal made a lateral movement, and ran broadside
against the fence. Ichabod, whose fears increased with the
delay, jerked the reins on the other side, and kicked lustily
with the contrary foot : it was all in vain ; his steed started, it
is true, but it was only to plunge to the opposite side of the
road into a thicket of brambles and alder-bushes. The schoolmaster now bestowed both whip and heel upon the starveling
ribs of old Gunpowder, who dashed forwards, snuffling and
snarting, but came to a stand just by the bridge, with a sud-
dennesss that had nearly sent his rider sprawling over his
head. Just at this moment a plashy tramp by the side of the
bridge caught the sensitive ear of Ichabod. In the dark
shadow of the grove, on the margin of the brook, he beheld
something huge, misshapen, black and towering. It stirred
not, but seemed gathered up in the gloom, like some gigantic
monster ready to spring upon the traveller.

The hair of the affrighted pedagogue rose upon his head
with terror. What was to be done ? To turn and fly was now
too late ; and besides, what chance was there of escaping
ghost or goblin, if such it was, which could ride upon the
wings of the wind ? Summoning up, therefore, a show of
courage, he demanded in stammering accents — "Who are
you ?" He received no reply. He repeated his demand in a
still more agitated voice. Still there was no answer. Once
more he cudgelled the sides of the inflexible Gunpowder, and
shutting his eyes, broke forth with involuntary fervor into a
psalm tune. Just then the shadowy object of alarm put itself
in motion, and with a scramble and a bound, stood at once in

the middle of the road. Though the night was dark and dismal, yet the form of the unknown might now in some degree be ascertained. He appeared to be a horseman of large dimensions, and mounted on a black horse of powerful frame. He made no offer of molestation or sociability, but kept aloof on one side of the road, jogging along on the blind side of old Gunpowder, who had now got over his fright and waywardness.

Ichabod, who had no relish for this strange midnight companion, and bethought himself of the adventure of Brom Bones with the galloping Hessian, now quickened his steed, in hopes of leaving him behind. The stranger, however, quickened his horse to an equal pace. Ichabod pulled up, and fell into a walk, thinking to lag behind—the other did the same. His heart began to sink within him; he endeavored to resume his psalm tune, but his parched tongue clove to the roof of his mouth, and he could not utter a stave. There was something in the moody and dogged silence of this pertinacious companion, that was mysterious and appalling. It was soon fearfully accounted for. On mounting a rising ground, which brought the figure of his fellow-traveller in relief against the sky, gigantic in height, and muffled in a cloak, Ichabod was horror struck, on perceiving that he was headless! but his horror was still more increased, on observing that the head, which should have rested on his shoulders, was carried before him on the pommel of his saddle! His terror rose to desperation; he rained a shower of kicks and blows upon Gunpowder, hoping, by a sudden movement, to give his companion the slip—but the spectre started full jump with him. Away, then, they dashed through thick and thin; stones flying and sparks flashing at every bound. Ichabod's flimsy garments fluttered in the air, as he stretched his long lank body away over his horse's head, in the eagerness of his flight.

They had now reached the road which turns off to Sleepy Hollow; but Gunpowder, who seemed possessed with a demon, instead of keeping up it, made an opposite turn and plunged headlong down hill to the left. This road leads through a sandy hollow, shaded by trees for about a quarter of a mile, where it crosses the bridge famous in goblin story; and just beyond swells the green knoll on which stands the whitewashed church.

As yet the panic of the steed had given his unskilful rider an apparent advantage in the chase; but just as he had got half-way through the hollow, the girths of the saddle gave way, and he felt it slipping from under him. He seized it by the pommel, and endeavored to hold it firm, but in vain; and had just time to save himself by clasping old Gunpowder round the neck, when the saddle fell to the earth, and he heard it trampled under foot by his pursuer. For a moment the terror of Hans Van Ripper's wrath passed across his mind—for it was his Sunday saddle; but this was no time for petty fears; the goblin was hard on his haunches; and (unskilful rider that he was!) he had much ado to maintain his seat; sometimes slipping on one side, sometimes on another, and sometimes jolted on the high ridge of his horse's backbone, with a violence that he verily feared would cleave him asunder.

An opening in the trees now cheered him with the hopes that the church bridge was at hand. The wavering reflection of a silver star in the bosom of the brook told him that he was not mistaken. He saw the walls of the church dimly glaring under the trees beyond. He recollected the place where Brom Bones' ghostly competitor had disappeared. "If I can but reach that bridge," thought Ichabod, "I am safe."[1] Just then he heard the black steed panting and blowing close behind him; he even fancied that he felt his hot breath. Another convulsive kick in the ribs, and old Gunpowder sprang upon the bridge; he thundered over the resounding planks; he gained the opposite side, and now Ichabod cast a look behind to see if his pursuer should vanish, according to rule, in a

---

[1] Ghosts and evil spirits, according to the superstition, cannot pass running water.

flash of fire and brimstone. Just then he saw the goblin rising in his stirrups, and in the very act of hurling his head at him. Ichabod endeavored to dodge the horrible missile, but too late. It encountered his cranium with a tremendous crash—he was tumbled headlong into the dust, and Gunpowder, the black steed, and the goblin rider, passed by like a whirlwind.

The next morning the old horse was found without his saddle, and with the bridle under his feet, soberly cropping the grass at his master's gate. Ichabod did not make his appearance at breakfast; dinner-hour came, but no Ichabod. The boys assembled at the school-house, and strolled idly about the banks of the brook; but no schoolmaster. Hans Van Ripper now began to feel some uneasiness about the fate of poor Ichabod, and his saddle. An inquiry was set on foot, and after diligent investigation they came upon his traces. In one part of the road leading to the church, was found the saddle, trampled in the dirt; the tracks of horses' hoofs deeply dented in the road, and, evidently at furious speed, were traced to the bridge, beyond which, on the bank of a broad part of the brook, where the water ran deep and black, was found the hat of the unfortunate Ichabod, and close beside it a shattered pumpkin.

The brook was searched, but the body of the schoolmaster was not to be discovered. Hans Van Ripper, as executor of his estate, examined the bundle which contained all his worldly effects. They consisted of two shirts and a half; two stocks for the neck; a pair or two of worsted stockings; an old pair of corduroy small-clothes; a rusty razor; a book of psalm tunes full of dog's ears; and a broken pitch-pipe. As to the books and furniture of the school-house, they belonged to the community, excepting Cotton Mather's History of Witchcraft, a New England Almanac, and a book of dreams and fortune-telling; in which last was a sheet of foolscap much scribbled and blotted, by several fruitless attempts to make a copy of verses in honor of the heiress of Van Tassel. These magic books and the poetic scrawl were forthwith consigned to the flames by Hans Van Ripper; who, from that time forward, determined to send his children no more to school; observing that he never knew any good come of this same reading and writing. Whatever money the schoolmaster possessed, and he had received his quarter's pay but a day or two before, he must have had about his person at the time of his disappearance.

The mysterious event caused much speculation at the church on the following Sunday. Knots of gazers and gossips were collected in the churchyard, at the bridge, and at the spot where the hat and pumpkin had been found. The stories of Brouwer, of Bones, and a whole budget of others, were called to mind; and when they had diligently considered them all, and compared them with the symptoms of the present case, they shook their heads, and came to the conclusion, that Ichabod had been carried off by the galloping Hessian. As he was a bachelor, and in nobody's debt, nobody troubled his head any more about him; the school was removed to a different quarter of the Hollow, and another pedagogue reigned in his stead.

It is true, an old farmer, who had been down to New York on a visit several years after, and from whom this account of the ghostly adventure was received, brought home the intelligence that Ichabod Crane was still alive; that he had left the neighborhood partly through fear of the goblin and Hans Van Ripper, and partly in mortification at having been suddenly dismissed by the heiress; that he had changed his quarters to a distant part of the country; had kept school and studied law at the same time; had been admitted to the bar; turned politician; electioneered; written for the newspapers; and finally, had been made a Justice of the Ten Pound Court. Brom Bones, too, who, shortly after his rival's disappearance, conducted the blooming Katrina in triumph to the altar, was·

observed to look exceedingly knowing whenever the story of Ichabod was related, and always burst into a hearty laugh at the mention of the pumpkin; which led some to suspect that he knew more about the matter than he chose to tell.

The old country wives, however, who are the best judges of these matters, maintain to this day, that Ichabod was spirited away by supernatural means; and it is a favorite story often told about the neighborhood round the winter evening fire. The bridge became more than ever an object of superstitious awe; and that may be the reason why the road has been altered of late years, so as to approach the church by the border of the mill-pond. The school-house being deserted, soon fell to decay, and was reported to be haunted by the ghost of the unfortunate pedagogue; and the plough-boy, loitering homeward of a still summer evening, has often fancied his voice at a distance, chanting a melancholy psalm tune among the tranquil solitudes of Sleepy Hollow.

POSTSCRIPT,

FOUND IN THE HANDWRITING OF MR. KNICKERBOCKER.

THE preceding Tale is given, almost in the precise words in which I heard it related at a Corporation meeting of the ancient city of the Manhattoes, at which were present many of its sagest and most illustrious burghers. The narrator was a pleasant, shabby, gentlemanly old fellow in pepper-and-salt clothes, with a sadly humorous face; and one whom I strongly suspected of being poor,—he made such efforts to be entertaining. When his story was concluded there was much laughter and approbation, particularly from two or three deputy aldermen, who had been asleep the greater part of the time. There was, however, one tall, dry-looking old gentleman, with beetling eye-brows, who maintained a grave and rather severe face throughout; now and then folding his arms, inclining his head, and looking down upon the floor, as if turning a doubt over in his mind. He was one of your wary men, who never laugh but upon good grounds—when they have reason and the law on their side. When the mirth of the rest of the company had subsided, and silence was restored, he leaned one arm on the elbow of his chair, and sticking the other a-kimbo, demanded, with a slight but exceedingly sage motion of the head, and contraction of the brow, what was the moral of the story, and what it went to prove.

The story-teller, who was just putting a glass of wine to his lips, as a refreshment after his toils, paused for a moment, looked at his inquirer with an air of infinite deference, and lowering the glass slowly to the table, observed that the story was intended most logically to prove :—

"That there is no situation in life but has its advantages and pleasures—provided we will but take a joke as we find it :

"That, therefore, he that runs races with goblin troopers, is likely to have rough riding of it :

"Ergo, for a country schoolmaster to be refused the hand of a Dutch heiress, is a certain step to high preferment in the state."

The cautious old gentleman knit his brows tenfold closer after this explanation, being sorely puzzled by the ratiocination of the syllogism ;[1] while, methought, the one in pepper-and-salt eyed him with something of a triumphant leer. At length he observed, that all this was very well, but still he thought the story a little on the extravagant—there were one or two points on which he had his doubts :

"Faith, sir," replied the story-teller, "as to that matter, I don't believe one-half of it myself."

D. K.

---

[1] Two statements (called premises) and a third inferred from them (called the conclusion) make a syllogism. The two premises must be connected with each other. Of course, the three sentences in the text, although stated as though they were an argument, have nothing to do with each other at all.

◦ Standard ◦ Literature ◦ Series ◦

Works of standard authors for supplementary reading in schools—complete selections or abridgments—with introductions and explanatory notes. Single numbers, 64 to 128 pages, stiff paper sides 12½ cents, cloth 20 cents ; double numbers, 160 to 224 pages, stiff paper sides 20 cents, cloth 30 cents. Paper edition, yearly subscription, twelve numbers, $1.75, prepaid.

CONTENTS OF THE FIRST TWENTY-FOUR (24) NUMBERS, ARRANGED BY COUNTRIES AND AUTHORS

Starred numbers are DOUBLE. All the works are complete, or contain complete selections, except those marked "abr."

American Authors

COOPER—The Spy, No. 1, single (abr.), 128 pp. *The Pilot, No. 2 (abr.), 181 pp. *The Deerslayer, No. 8 (abr.), 160 pp.

DANA, R. H., Jr.—*Two Years Before the Mast, No. 19 (abr.), 173 pp.

HAWTHORNE—Twice-Told Tales, No. 15, single, complete selections, 128 pp.: The Village Uncle, The Ambitious Guest, Mr. Higginbotham's Catastrophe, A Rill from the Town Pump, The Great Carbuncle, David Swan, Dr. Heidegger's Experiment, Peter Goldthwaite's Treasure, The Threefold Destiny, Old Esther Dudley.

A Wonder-Book, for Girls and Boys, No. 16, single, complete selections, 121 pp.: The Golden Touch, The Paradise of Children, The Three Golden Apples, The Miraculous Pitcher.

The Snow-Image and other Twice-Told Tales, No. 20, single, complete selections, 121 pp.: The Snow-Image, The Great Stone Face, Little Daffydowndilly, The Vision of the Fountain, The Seven Vagabonds, Little Annie's Ramble, The Prophetic Pictures.

IRVING—The Alhambra, No. 4, single, complete selections, 128 pp.: Palace of the Alhambra; Alhamar, the Founder of the Alhambra; Yusef Abul Hagig, the Finisher of the Alhambra; Panorama from the Tower of Comares; Legend of the Moor's Legacy; Legend of the Rose of the Alhambra; The Governor and the Notary; Governor Manco and the Soldier; Legend of Two Discreet Statues; Legend of Don Munio Sancho de Hinojosa; The Legend of the Enchanted Soldier.

The Sketch-Book, No. 17, single, complete selections, 121 pp.: The Author's Account of Himself, The Broken Heart, The Spectre Bridegroom, Rural Life in England, The Angler, John Bull, The Christmas Dinner, Stratford-on-Avon.

Knickerbocker Stories, No. 23, single, complete selections, 140 pp.: I. Broek, or the Dutch Paradise; II. From Knickerbocker's New York, (a) New Amsterdam under Van Twiller, (b) How William the Testy Defended the City, (c) Peter Stuyvesant's Voyage up the Hudson; III. Wolfert's Roost; IV. The Storm Ship; V. Rip Van Winkle; VI. A Legend of Sleepy Hollow.

KENNEDY, J. P.—*Horse-Shoe Robinson, a Tale of the Revolution, No. 10 (abr.), 192 pp.

LONGFELLOW—Evangeline, a Tale of Acadie, No. 21, single, complete, 102 pp.

English Authors

BULWER-LYTTON—*Harold, the Last of the Saxon Kings, No. 12 (abr.), 160 pp.

BYRON—The Prisoner of Chillon and Other Poems, No. 11, single, complete selections, 128 pp.: The Prisoner of Chillon, Mazeppa, Childe Harold.

DICKENS—Christmas Stories, No. 5, single (abr.), 142 pp.: A Christmas Carol, The Cricket on the Hearth, The Child's Dream of a Star.
　　Little Nell (from Old Curiosity Shop), No. 22, single (abr.), 123 pp.
　　Paul Dombey (from Dombey and Son), No. 14, single (abr.), 128 pp.

SCOTT—*Ivanhoe, No. 24 (abr.), 180 pp.　*Kenilworth, No. 7 (abr.), 164 pp.　*Lady of the Lake, No. 9, complete, 192 pp.　Rob Roy, No. 3, single (abr.), 130 pp.

SWIFT—Gulliver's Travels, Voyages to Lilliput and Brobdingnag, No. 13, single (abr.), 128 pp.

TENNYSON—Enoch Arden and Other Poems, No. 6, single, complete selections, 110 pp.: Enoch Arden; The Coming of Arthur; The Passing of Arthur; Columbus; The May Queen; New Year's Eve; Conclusion; Dora; The Charge of the Light Brigade; The Defence of Lucknow; Lady Clare; Break, Break, Break; The Brook; Bugle Song; Widow and Child; The Days That Are No More; I Envy Not; Oh, Yet We Trust; Ring Out, Wild Bells; Crossing the Bar (Tennyson's last poem).

French Authors

HUGO, VICTOR—*Ninety-Three, No. 18 (abr.), 157 pp.

Grading.—For History Classes: Spy, Pilot, Deerslayer, Horse-Shoe Robinson, Knickerbocker Stories, Harold, Kenilworth, Rob Roy, Ivanhoe, Ninety-Three, Alhambra. Geography: Two Years Before the Mast. English Literature: Evangeline, Lady of the Lake, Enoch Arden, Prisoner of Chillon, Sketch-Book. Lower Grammar Grades: Christmas Stories, Little Nell, Paul Dombey, Gulliver's Travels, Twice-Told Tales. Primary Grades: Wonder-Book, Snow-Image.

Correspondence is invited. Special discounts on this series on all orders from schools and dealers. Address

University ⁕ Publishing ⁕ Company
Educational Publishers
43-45-47 East Tenth St., New York
BOSTON: 352 Washington St.　NEW ORLEANS: 714-716 Canal St.

WHAT PROMINENT EDUCATORS SAY

OF THE

STANDARD LITERATURE SERIES

W. T. Harris, *Commissioner of Education, Washington, D. C.* " I have examined very carefully one of the abridgments from Walter Scott, and I would not have believed the essentials of the story could have been retained with so severe an abridgment. But the story thus abridged has kept its interest and all of the chief threads of the plot. I am very glad that the great novels of Walter Scott are in course of publication by your house in such a form that school children, and older persons as yet unfamiliar with Walter Scott, may find an easy introduction. To read Walter Scott's novels is a large part of a liberal education, but his discourses on the history of the times and his disquisitions on motives render his stories too hard for the person of merely elementary education. But if one can interest himself in the plot, and skip these learned passages, he may, on a second reading, be able to grasp the whole novel. Hence I look to such abridgments as you have made for a great extension of Walter Scott's usefulness."

Charles W. Eliot, *President Harvard University, Cambridge, Mass.* " I have looked over your abbreviations of ' The Pilot' and ' The Spy,' and think them very well adapted to grammar school use. I should think the principle might be applied to novels which have no historical setting, and the famous books of adventure."

William H. Maxwell, *Superintendent of Public Instruction, Brooklyn, N. Y.* " I take great pleasure in commending to those who are seeking for good reading in the schools, the Standard Literature Series. The editors of the series have struck out a new line in the preparation of literature for schools. They have taken great works of fiction and poetry, and so edited them as to omit what is beyond the comprehension, or what would weary the attention, of children in the higher grades of elementary schools. The books are published in good form and at so low a rate as to bring literature that too seldom finds its way into the schools, not only within the comprehension, but within the purchasing power, of all school children."

E. H. Davis, *Superintendent, Chelsea, Mass.* "I have read through with much interest the copies of your Standard Literature Series, and have placed several of them on our list of approved supplementary readers. The wonder is that any house can offer such books at so small cost."

C. F. Boyden, *Superintendent, Taunton, Mass.* "I am thoroughly convinced that the *real reading* of all our pupils should be standard literature. I think your Standard Literature Series well selected and well adapted for this work."

Mason S. Stone, *State Superintendent, Montpelier, Vermont.* "Admirably adapted to our public schools."

G. A. Southworth, *Superintendent, Somerville, Mass.* "I have examined copies of your Standard Literature Series with interest and pleasure. The subjects selected are excellent and the plan of the series commends itself. The low price brings the books within easy reach."

Eugene Bouton, *Superintendent, Pittsfield, Mass.* "The ideal reading would take the masterpieces complete. Lack of time and money, however, must usually make the attainment of this ideal in many cases impracticable. In all such cases your Standard Literature Series seems a happy solution of the greatest good attainable under existing conditions."

Wm. H. Huse, *Principal Hallsville School, Manchester, N. H.* "I have examined the Standard Literature Series and can hardly use language too strong in praise of both the books and the plan on which they are arranged and issued, as well as the motive that brings them out."

Franklin Carter, *President Williams College, Williamstown, Mass.* "I think the idea a good one of making the reading of our schools cover some such fine stories as are embodied in the Standard Literature Series. The abbreviations are necessary, and I judge are well done. The notes are certainly discriminating and helpful."

S. T. Dutton, *Superintendent, Brookline, Mass.* "I am glad to say that I have been much pleased with the form and the execution of the Standard Literature Series. The selections thus far have been excellent and the books are attractively constructed."

Thos. M. Balliet, *Superintendent, Springfield, Mass.* "I like your series of the classics so far as I have seen the different numbers."

UNIVERSITY PUBLISHING COMPANY
43-47 East 10th Street, New York